KU-018-297

THE MANUSCRIPT KILLER

When Detective Inspector Drizzle receives a mysterious message from elderly recluse Matthew Trevelyn imploring him to visit the next day, as he is in fear of his life, Drizzle sets out straight away. Delayed by a punctured tyre, however, he arrives at the country house to discover he's too late: Trevelyn has been brutally murdered — strangled by a silk scarf belonging to his niece. Her boyfriend had been thrown out the previous night after a raging quarrel with Trevelyn — but is he the true culprit? Thus begins Drizzle's strangest case . . .

NOEL LEE

THE MANUSCRIPT KILLER

Complete and Unabridged

LINFORD
Leicester

First published in Great Britain

First Linford Edition
published 2019

Copyright © 1940 by Noel Lee
Copyright © 2018 by Jan Layton-Smith

A catalogue record for this book is available
from the British Library.

ISBN 978–1–4448–4145–9

1

A Beautiful Woman Faints

The florid-faced landlord of the Barrel Inn pushed a foaming tankard across the beer-stained counter, and leaned heavily towards his customer.

''Ave you 'eard,' he whispered hoarsely, 'about 'im an' Mr. Trevelyn?'

The other looked round, followed Mr. Balmer's gaze through the noisy crowd of villagers that congested the low-timbered bar-parlour, and saw the broad shoulders of a young man disappear through the doorway.

'You forget,' he remarked as he turned back and reached for his beer, 'that I only arrived in Enderby approximately five minutes ago.' He raised the tankard to his lips, and drank the contents with the relish of one who enjoys his beer with no mean satisfaction. 'Who is he?'

''Im?' Mr. Balmer nodded in the

direction of the door. ''Im who's just gone out? That's Mr. Manton. But it ain't 'is fault.'

'Really?' The stranger transferred his gaze from the depths of his tankard to the round, jovial face of the speaker. 'Go on.'

Mr. Balmer stretched his hand for a nearby glass, which he proceeded to polish with the vigour that only innkeepers of long standing seem to have attained.

'Course, sir, I'd forgotten you was a stranger. Naturally you wouldn't know anything about Mr. Trevelyn. Not,' he added somewhat wistfully, 'that we down 'ere know much about 'im if it comes to that. Very reticent 'e is — very reticent.' He repeated the word with obvious relish, as if he possessed some special liking for it — as indeed he did. ''Tain't often 'e comes into the village, you know. Only of a Sunday when 'e goes to church.'

The customer nodded, and placed his half-drained tankard on the counter. He found himself taking an unusual interest in Mr. Balmer's prominent nose, and guessed from its cherry-like redness that the villagers of Enderby were not the only consumers of the Barrel's excellent ale.

'Bit of a recluse, eh?' he asked.

Mr. Balmer scratched the small bare patch that crowned the top of his bullet-like head, and frowned.

'Well, sir, I wouldn't call 'im that exactly. 'E don't lock 'imself up and refuse to see nobody, like them people you sometimes read about in the papers. 'E 'as plenty of visitors, but they're all 'is special friends, if you know what I mean. There's Major Tilson up at the 'all. 'E goes. Then there's that Mrs. Garvice. A widder, she is. Lost 'er 'usband in a motor accident last year, but do you know, sir — ' He became amusingly confidential. ' — it's surprising 'ow quickly that gal recovered . . . Then there's the vicar. Oh, and yes, there's young Mr. Manton. Doesn't go to see the old man, though. It's Miss Trevelyn 'e goes for.' The listener nodded again, and his hand sought the capacious pocket of his thick overcoat, from which he drew an exceedingly battered pipe.

'So he's got a daughter, has he?' he asked, as he stuffed tobacco into the well-burned bowl.

The innkeeper shook his head and eyed the pipe thoughtfully. Perhaps he thought the customer could do with a new one.

'She ain't 'is daughter, sir,' he replied. 'Niece, I think. Only came to live with 'im three or four years ago. Gawky young thing of about sixteen, then, and a real wildcat she was, too. Used to drive the 'ousekeeper frantic, I believe. But she's quietened down now, though, and there's not a nicer lady anywhere. Don't wonder Mr. Manton wants to marry 'er.'

'Oh, so Mr. Manton wants to marry her, eh?'

'Yes, sir. An' that's what all the trouble's about. Shame, I call it, an' young Mr. Manton bein' such a decent young feller, too.' Mr. Balmer paused, and examined his glass in the true proprietorial style. 'Course the lady's only young, I'll grant you, but what I says is this: if she really wants to marry young Manton, why shouldn't she? 'E ain't done nobody any 'arm, an' 'e's a dang sight better'n some I could mention.' Obviously satisfied with the result of his labours, he replaced the glass on the counter and reached for another.

'I see,' said the customer. He applied a match to his pipe, thereby adding a huge cloud of smoke to the already thick atmosphere of the bar. 'And who, may I ask, is Mr. Manton?'

'Meanter — meanter say you — you've never 'eard of 'im, sir?' asked the innkeeper in a tone that lost most of its incredulity through a series of spluttering coughs. Even Mr. Balmer, used as he was to tobacco of nearly every variety, could not help being affected by this stranger's obnoxious mixture. 'Why, I thought that everyone who read them there mystery stories knew Phillip Manton?'

'Really?' The other flicked the spent match into one of the many spittoons that littered the sanded floor. 'Well, here's one who hasn't heard of him. I never read thrillers.'

'Of course, there's them that likes a bit of adventure, an' there's them that don't,' allowed Mr. Balmer, whose chief relaxation (besides generously sampling his own well-conditioned ale) was to bury himself in as many 'blood and thunders' as Mr. Gregg's tiny newsagent's shop could supply. 'That's a matter o' taste, I suppose. But if you don't do much in the way of readin', you won't know Mr. Manton. 'E's one of them writer chaps, you know. Quite good, 'e is, though 'e's only very young. Took Briar Cottage 'bout sixteen months ago, an' now 'e's one of the most pop'lar young fellers in the village. Everybody likes 'im — includin' Miss Trevelyn.' He smiled. 'Grand pair they are, too. It's a shame the old man not lettin' 'em get married as they want to.'

'Oh, yes, you said that was the trouble. But surely if this Mr. Manton of yours is such a fine upright young chap, popular with the village lads and all that sort of thing, why shouldn't she marry him? I mean, what has Miss — er — Trevelyn's uncle got against him?'

'That's just the point, sir,' replied the innkeeper, once more leaning over the counter in spite of the heavy haze of tobacco smoke that still hung there. 'That's where all the mystery comes in.' Mr. Balmer seemed rather keen on mystery. 'As far as anybody knows, 'e's never 'ad anythin' against 'im — not up to last night, any'ow. It's 'im turning all of a sudden-like that's upset Miss Margery so much. In an awful way, she is. You see, Mr. Manton used to go up to the 'ouse quite often, but when 'e went last night . . . ' Mr. Balmer paused. 'Of course, sir,' he added, hastily, 'I only know the facts as I got 'em from young Joe Rodgers. 'E's the milkman, you know. That's 'im over there.' He nodded across the smoke-laden bar, but the loquacious Mr. Rodgers was hidden by a group of excited dart players.

'Anyway, accordin' to what 'e says, there was a rare rumpus then. Turned Mr. Manton out of the 'ouse, 'e did — 'im who's never done no 'arm to nobody — then ordered Miss Margery never to see 'im again. Carried on somethin' awful, I 'ear.' He sighed. 'An' all because of 'em wantin' to get married.'

The customer took his pipe from his lips and finished his beer.

'Well, that's happened more than once in history,' he remarked as he fumbled in his pocket for some loose change. 'They say the course of true love never runs straight. Personally I've never had any experience in that direction.' He placed a two-shilling piece on the counter, and Mr. Balmer took it for the drink. 'My troubles go a bit deeper than that.'

Mr. Balmer nodded sympathetically, though he hadn't the least idea what the other was getting at. The stranger pocketed the change, thanked him, and moved towards the door.

'Oh, by the way.' He stopped in the act of donning his hat. 'I nearly forgot. Can you direct me to Friar's Lodge?'

The innkeeper stared.

'Friar — Friar's Lodge, did you say, sir?'

The other nodded.

'But — but that's where Mr. Trevelyn lives . . . '

'Yes.' The man smiled. 'I'm quite aware of that. You see — ' He became suddenly conscious from the indignant grunts of his fellow customers that he was standing in the way of the dart board, and he hastily concluded the conversation. 'Never mind, I'll find it. Good night.'

Apologetically, he edged his way through

the crowd, and the game continued. A few seconds later there sounded the clash of a door, followed almost immediately by the sudden roar of a car that was lost in the chatter of the customers as it sped down the street.

Mr. Balmer, who was left staring at the swinging doors of the bar-parlour, scratched his head and pursed his lips in one expressive exclamation:

'Well, I'll be blowed!'

★   ★   ★

It was about ten minutes later that the man in the Bentley Sports Tourer arrived in the vicinity of Friar's Lodge. Thanks to the somewhat lengthy instructions of a local police-constable whom he had met while on his beat, the stranger had been able to find the correct road without any real difficulty — and certainly without the help of that very astonished gentleman, Mr. Balmer.

The night was cold and damp, and the rough country road crunched softly under the pressure of the tyres. A watery moon had made its bedraggled appearance from behind a bank of heavy cloud, and the driver noted a few spots of rain on the windscreen.

Friar's Lodge stood well back from the roadway, almost hidden in the thickly growing trees that surrounded it. He thumbed the electric horn, swung the car through the open gateway, and drove slowly up the gravelled drive. It was an old house — a very old house, with thick patches of creeper running over the grey stone walls. It did much to soften the harsh corners, but even then it looked strangely gaunt and forbidding.

He brought the car to a standstill before three wide steps that led up to an arch-shaped portico. He didn't know why, but as he looked at that house he had a strange feeling that there was something wrong with it. Of course it was imagination — it must be. The house was dark, and the heavy grey clouds that were obscuring the moon overhead were making it look darker. Yet the only sign of life was a tiny shaft of light that pierced the darkness from between two closely drawn curtains in a downstairs window.

He glanced at the clock on the dashboard of the car. It was nearly half-past eight. What an unearthly hour to arrive. Mr. Trevelyn must have given up hope ages since. Still, he'd made the journey as quickly as he could, and if it hadn't been for that infernal puncture he'd have been here hours ago.

He had switched off the engine, and was just getting out of the car when he heard it.

It was a scream — faint, but definitely a scream. It came from the house, and it was of such a timbre that he knew it could only have come from a woman.

He bounded up the steps with a swiftness that was truly surprising for a man of his shortness. His hand sought the heavy iron knocker that ornamented the huge door, and with all the strength he could muster beat a thundering tattoo on the weather-beaten oak.

The sound echoed and re-echoed through the length and breadth of the house, and died away in a silence that left him with a vague feeling of doubt. He had heard it . . . he was sure he had . . . and yet there seemed to be no one at home — despite that light in the lower window.

He seized the knocker again and sent another crash reverberating through the stillness. This time his efforts were rewarded, for as the last echo died away, he heard the sharp tap-tap of feet as someone came hurrying across a stone-flagged hall. It seemed an eternity before the harsh grating of a bolt announced the door being opened, and a few seconds later the heavy door swung inwards, revealing a small figure framed between the jambs.

It was a woman; but all he could see of her in the sudden glare of the hall was that she was intensely beautiful. It needed no second thought to tell him that this was the Margery Trevelyn he had been hearing so much about; she was too refined and cultured for a maidservant. But she was frightened — badly fright-ened — and there seemed little doubt that the scream had come from her. Her face was deadly pale, and one hand was clutched tightly at her breast. He spoke.

'Good evening. Sorry if I startled you. My name's Drizzle. I've called to see Mr. Trevelyn.'

He saw her pretty face, shadowy and indistinct as it was, turn an even whiter pallor than before, and her lips trembled as she strove to say something by way of an answer. Finally she spoke, but her voice came only in a whisper.

'I — I'm afraid you can't. He's dead. Who are you?'

The man was plainly startled.

'I've told you. My name's Drizzle — Detective Inspector Drizzle of New Scotland Yard. But what — '

He didn't say any more, for she had collapsed in a dead faint at his feet.

2

The Broken Wire

To say that Mr. Drizzle was surprised would be to express his feelings by a term inadequate to the situation. As one of the most energetic men at Scotland Yard, he was used to surprises — no one more than he; but never had he anticipated anything like this. He knew now that his initial impression of Friar's Lodge was correct. There *was* something wrong, and what it was he meant to find out. He did not, however, waste time in idle conjecture; he stooped, lifted the frail figure in two powerful arms, and stepped into the hall.

It was a large, gloomy place with a wide staircase beginning at the far end. A plain oak table and two benches ran down the centre, and a number of small mats covered the flags at varying intervals. The walls were richly panelled in dark oak, and several doors opened off to the left and right. A dim lamp suspended from the raftered ceiling cast a sombre glow over the scene.

He stood undecided for a couple of seconds, then made with his burden for the nearest door. He put his foot against it, and it responded to the touch.

The light was on, and the room he passed into was pleasant. Drawing room, probably. His eyes caught a large divan set in the bay of the heavily curtained window, and he crossed to it and laid the woman down. With sudden inspiration, he arranged a cushion beneath her head, then threw off his hat and knelt beside her.

She was very beautiful — he'd noticed that before — with the most gorgeous mass of dark brown hair he'd ever seen. If he'd been guessing, he'd have taken her to be twenty-four or five — and been hopelessly wrong. This modern generation was so confoundedly confusing. According to Mr. Balmer's statement, she must be just on twenty.

He wasn't used to faints, especially

fainting women, and he hadn't the least idea what to do. He remembered vaguely that patting the hands sometimes did the trick. He tried it, without any real conviction, and was surprised at the result. Almost immediately she showed signs of coming round, and a few seconds later she sighed and opened her eyes. He spoke in a voice that was strangely soothing.

'Lie still, Miss Trevelyn. You're all right.'

She disregarded his advice, struggled hastily into a sitting position, and passed a shaky hand over her forehead.

'I'm frightfully sorry. It was stupid of me.' She smiled tremulously. 'I don't think I've fainted since the time I twisted my ankle at the house sports. But . . . ' She looked puzzled. 'How did you know my name?'

It was his turn to smile. 'I didn't think you were one of the servants, you know.' They both rose. 'By the way, where *are* the servants?'

She turned to him with an expression of complete bewilderment on her features. 'I — I don't know.'

'You don't know? But surely — ' He gave her a sharp glance. 'Was it you who screamed?'

She swayed unsteadily, and her face lost most of the colour it had regained. Mr. Drizzle caught her arm.

'Sorry. I shouldn't have asked you like that. It was you, wasn't it?' She nodded. 'I thought so. Now tell me, why did you scream?'

'I couldn't help it. I saw him. It — it was awful.' He felt her slim young body shaking. 'He's dead, I think.'

He nodded. He only asked one question. 'Where is he?'

'In the study.'

He pressed her arm. 'Show me.'

With obvious reluctance, she allowed herself to be propelled towards the door. They reached the hall in silence, and she indicated a partly opened door on the other side.

'In — there.'

Mr. Drizzle crossed to the room and stood on the threshold. One glance was sufficient to tell him that the man within was dead. He lay face upwards near the open French window, with a small silk scarf pulled tightly round his neck. His face, deep and lined with age, was ghastly to behold. There was little wonder the woman had screamed. His eyes protruded like two grotesque marbles from his lean grey head, and glistened horribly in the diffused light of the lamp. His mouth was wide open, and his hands clutched desperately at the scarf that encircled his throat.

Drizzle felt a horrible choking sensation, and averted his gaze from the scene. Strangled — every ounce of life's breath choked from his wiry body by that gaudy remnant of silk that was pulled so tightly round his throat.

He turned, and was surprised to find the woman at his elbow. Hastily he pulled the door to.

'He's — he's dead, isn't he?'

Mr. Drizzle nodded. She seemed to have collected most of her scattered composure, but unshed tears sparkled in her deep brown eyes. He saw that she was on the point of another collapse, and gently he led her to the drawing room.

'You'd better sit down,' he said, 'and try to keep as calm as you can.'

She uttered a little gasp, and flopped dully into the nearest chair. Mr. Drizzle peeled off his coat and threw it over the divan.

'Now,' he said, turning to her, 'you've had a pretty hefty shock, and I don't want to distress you more than necessary, but you must answer my questions. That — that person in there; he's Matthew Trevelyn, isn't he?'

She nodded.

'Thank you. And you, I suppose, are his niece?' It was more of a statement than a question, and she nodded again. Speech seemed an intolerable ordeal. 'Right. Now, Miss Trevelyn, perhaps you'll be able to tell me where all the servants are?'

'I can't. I — I don't know.'

'What do you mean, you don't know?'

'Simply what I say. I have no more idea than you as to where they have got to.'

Mr. Drizzle sighed.

'Perhaps you'd better begin at the beginning,' he suggested. 'Then we might get some idea what all this is about. How long have you been in the house?'

'Only about five minutes before — before I found him,' she replied haltingly. 'You see, I've been out most of the day; went out soon after lunch, and had tea with a friend. When I came back to dinner I expected to find everything as usual. When I tried the front door, however, it was fastened, and I had to knock. I didn't get a reply, so naturally I supposed that Grasset hadn't heard. I was very annoyed when I knocked again and received no answer. I couldn't imagine what had happened to them, so I decided to try to find my way round to the kitchen entrance. The moon was out, but it was still very dark, and there was no light in the kitchen. I went in and called for Mrs. Mimms — she's the housekeeper, you know; but . . . she wasn't there. I called for Ann, but she wasn't about, either. And there was no sign of Grasset. It — it was so mystifying. The house seemed deserted.'

Mr. Drizzle nodded. She continued: 'I didn't know what to make of it. I thought that perhaps for some particular reason everyone might have gone upstairs, so I went up to see. I looked into most of the bedrooms, but — there was nobody. I came down to uncle's study. I felt sure he'd be there if he was in the house at all, and — ' She choked. 'He was. I opened the door, but the room was in darkness, so I switched on the light, and — saw him. I — I screamed. Oh, it was horrible.' She gave a little shudder, as if she were trying to shake off the memory. 'How long I stood there, I couldn't tell you. It seemed like hours. Then — then I heard you knock. You know the rest.'

'I see.' He acknowledged her story with another nod. 'Thank you very much, Miss Trevelyn. Now tell me, when was it you last saw your uncle?'

'Last night.'

'Not this morning, then?'

'No.' She had her answer ready. 'You see, he had breakfast in bed. I gathered he wasn't feeling too well. He told the maid he had caught a cold, so he'd stay in for the morning. He had lunch in bed, too.'

'Weren't you rather worried about him?'

'No more than usual. He was very susceptible to colds and didn't believe in taking chances. He remained in bed at the first sign of one. They generally passed off in a day.'

'I see. You didn't go up to him, then?'

'N-no.' Her tone was hesitant. 'I was out during the afternoon. I never saw him till — till about ten minutes ago. I never dreamed that — that — ' Most of her previous fear began to return, and she sprang from her seat and confronted him in tearful bewilderment. 'Oh, tell me, what does it all mean? Who are you, and what are you doing here?'

Mr. Drizzle grasped her by the wrists and held her steadily. 'I told you my name. My business here is quite legitimate, but I'd rather you didn't ask questions now; I want you to answer them. A serious crime has been committed, but it's no good you getting upset. Your uncle has been murdered, and the only way you can help is to do as I say.'

It sounded brutal, but it had the desired effect. He released her, and he knew now that she was completely herself, and fully alive to the gravity of the situation.

'I'm sorry,' she apologized. 'I'm in a daze yet, and hardly able to understand what's happened. Where are Mrs. Mimms, Grasset, and the others?' She started. 'You don't think that — '

'That they're responsible for this crime and have bolted during your absence?' He smiled. 'No, I should hardly think that — though it may just be possible. But I think it's time we informed the police, you know. You have a telephone?'

'Yes, in the hall. I'll show you.'

She led him to a small table by the side of the stairs, and stood at his elbow as he put through the call. She watched his face intently as he lifted the receiver. She rather liked his looks, though at the same time she felt curiously frightened of him. She wondered what he was doing here, and what possible connection he could have with this horrible business. She shuddered. It was horrible — intensely horrible, and somehow, it all evaded her comprehension. Who could have done it? And why? Where was Grasset ... Ann ... Mrs.

Mimms . . . any of the staff? Questions flowed through her brain in an endless stream, each one giving rise to another, and serving to answer none of them. Then this man — this strange man . . . Scotland Yard he'd said, hadn't he . . . ?

She became suddenly aware that he had replaced the receiver, and was gazing at it thoughtfully.

'That's strange,' he muttered half to himself. 'Very strange.'

'What is?'

'I can't get through.'

'You can't get through? But — why not?' Her face was puzzled. 'The phone was in full working order this morning, I know. Ann rang up the village to order some groceries. Perhaps — perhaps you've not operated it right. I mean,' she added hastily, 'it's such a funny instrument. May I have a try? I understand it better than you.'

Mr. Drizzle stood aside without a word. His expression was curiously thoughtful, and he pulled at his lower lip. He nodded ponderously as Margery replaced the receiver and turned to him with a worried shake of her head.

'It's no use,' she confessed. 'You're right. The line is absolutely dead. I can't understand it.'

'I think I can, though.' And the stocky man sighed as he stooped and picked up the trailing lead wire. 'The flex has been cut,' he explained. 'Funny I never saw that at first.'

'Cut?' Alarm crept into Margery's voice again. 'But — but why should anyone want to do a thing like that?'

'There are lots of reasons,' replied Mr. Drizzle slowly, 'but I'll only give you one. This is a pretty lonely place, and the only link we have with the village, is — or rather, was — this telephone.'

'You mean — '

'It's pretty obvious, isn't it? There's some-one who doesn't want us to communicate with the police. That someone is danger-ous — he's the murderer, and if he thought we were a menace to his safe getaway . . . '

3

The Butler Tells His Story

For a few seconds Margery Trevelyn stared at Mr. Drizzle in wondering silence, then suddenly the truth dawned upon her.

'You mean,' she said with a little intake of breath, 'that whoever cut the wire did so to prevent us getting through to the police?'

'That,' replied Mr. Drizzle, 'seems to have been the idea, certainly. I wonder what you'd have done if I hadn't turned up? You'd have hurried down to the village yourself, wouldn't you?'

'Yes.' Margery hesitated, then nodded her assent. 'Yes, I suppose I should. At any rate, I shouldn't have stayed in the house after this. But — but if I *had* gone into the village, I should have had to go on foot, you know. You see, we haven't a car, and — '

'Of course,' broke in the inspector quickly. 'That explains it. That was why he cut the wire — and I think it is fairly obvious what he's done. Don't you see? He wanted you to fetch the police yourself, and waste as much time as you could in doing so. Oh yes, it was a simple idea, and I suppose if I hadn't turned up it would have worked admirably. The longer he succeeded in keeping the police off the scene, the more sure he was of a safe getaway.'

Margery nodded. 'Yes, I see that now. But . . . ' She paused and glanced helplessly at the telephone. 'What are we going to do?'

'With that?' Mr. Drizzle shrugged resignedly. 'Nothing. It may take us hours to find where the break is, and even then it may not be possible to mend it. I'll run down to the village myself shortly. Just now, however, I should like to have a look round. Before the local men take over, you know. I wonder — '

What it was he wondered Margery never knew, for he broke off in the middle of the sentence as from somewhere near at hand came a series of dull, irregular thuds. They were slow and laborious, and might, thought Mr. Drizzle after a few seconds, have been made by someone kicking. Margery looked at him in alarm.

'What is it?' she asked tremulously. 'It seems to be coming from the kitchen — '

The inspector held up a silencing finger, but even as they listened the sounds ceased.

'If the kitchen's through there, then you're right,' decided the stocky man suddenly. 'And unless I'm very much mistaken, it solves the problem of the missing servants, also. Come on.'

He was halfway along the short passage that ran by the side of the stairs before she had time to realize what he meant. She followed quickly on his heels, and caught up with him as he entered a large stone-flagged apartment. It was a high, roomy place with a massive white-topped table that occupied most of the centre, and which from its compelling bulk seemed to assume a lordly predominance over many articles of a smaller nature.

The thumping had begun again and was now quite distinct, and it was obvious that it emanated from the interior of the tall cupboard, which, together with a spotlessly clean cooking range, occupied most of the opposite wall. The inspector crossed the room in a couple of strides. There was a key in the lock, and Mr. Drizzle turned it and wrenched open the door.

In different circumstances, it might have been amusing. Huddled uncomfortably among a scattered pile of newspapers, which were apparently there for the purpose of lighting the kitchen fire, was the sombrely clad figure of a butler. He was bound hand and foot with lengths of thick clothes line, and a large yellow duster had been tied effectively across his mouth as a gag. He was twisting and turning in a vain attempt to free himself, but he ceased and cast a crimson face upwards as the door was flung open. He blinked painfully in the sudden light of the kitchen.

'Grasset!' exclaimed Margery in amazement. 'How on earth did you get there?'

'We'll know that presently,' grunted Mr. Drizzle, as the figure's only response was an unintelligible mumble. 'I think we'd better get him out first.'

The inspector showed not the least sign of astonishment, and it was evident that either he was able to exercise great control over his feelings, or he had expected something of the sort. With much puffing and blowing, he lifted the helpless figure out of the depths of the cupboard and sat him stiffly on a chair that Margery hastily brought forward. His fingers went to the knot in the duster, and a few seconds later the gag slipped to the floor.

'Thank you, sir,' gasped the butler breathlessly. 'That was — rather uncomfortable — while it lasted.'

With the aid of a convenient bread knife, the inspector had commenced operations on the ropes, and the man winced in pain as the circulation was restored to his cramped limbs.

Undoing the huge knots did not take the Scotland Yard man long. With the ropes lying in strands on the floor, he rose to his feet and regarded the butler carefully. He was a big broad-shouldered man with large, deep-set eyes and unkempt, overhanging eyebrows. His hair, thick and brown, flecked with faint streaks of grey, was long, and there was some semblance of the mid-Victorian side-whiskers that manservants of a few years ago seemed to favour. In age he might have been any-where between forty-five and fifty. There was no doubt, however, that he was remark-ably strong. Mr. Drizzle pondered on that point.

It was some moments before Grasset gained sufficient breath to speak, but when he did, Margery seized the opportunity to put to him a question that had been both-ering her as well as Mr. Drizzle for some time.

'Grasset,' she asked apprehensively, 'do you know where Ann and the others have got to? They seem to have disappeared completely.'

The butler looked up in surprise. 'Don't you know, miss? But, of course . . . ' His expression changed. ' . . . you won't. You were out when Mr. Trevelyn told us.'

'Told you what?' put in the Scotland Yard man sharply.

'That we could go to the fair, sir,' replied Grasset.

'Fair?' Margery sounded puzzled, then suddenly a look of enlightenment swept across her features. 'Oh, you mean the fair over at Helmthorpe?'

'Yes, miss, that's it.' The butler got to his feet. 'You see, there are only two more days of it, and Mr. Trevelyn thought we might care to go.'

'I see,' mused Mr. Drizzle. 'So that's the explanation, is it? And we thought . . . ' He frowned and rubbed his chin thoughtfully. 'But in that case, why didn't you go, too?'

'Me, sir?' If the butler wondered at this stranger's presence, and his authority to ask questions, he didn't show it. 'Well, to tell you the truth, sir, fairs are not much in my line, and anyway, I had rather a bad headache. I'd had a tiring day and I was looking forward to a quiet evening on my own.' He started as if a sudden thought struck him. 'I hope nothing has happened to Mr. Trevelyn. You've seen him, I suppose?'

'Oh yes, we've seen him,' replied the man from Scotland Yard slowly. 'But he isn't a very pleasant sight. He's dead.'

'Dead!' The inspector watched Grasset's face for the effect of this calm pronouncement. The butler slipped back into the chair, a look of horror passing over his saturnine countenance. 'Dead, did you say? My God! When — when did it happen?'

'I don't know,' said Margery in a very low voice. 'I found him about ten minutes ago. He — he was — '

'Strangled,' finished Mr. Drizzle, shortly. 'And it wasn't suicide.'

A period of tense silence followed upon this startling declaration. Grasset passed a shaky hand over his brow and licked his thick, dry lips. Horror and amazement were pictured in his lined face as he stared sightlessly at Mr. Drizzle. Then, with an effort, he pulled himself together and rose unsteadily to his feet. Save for a faint whiteness in his normally pallid cheeks, he was once more the perfect butler.

'I'm very sorry, miss. It must have been a terrible shock for you. If there is anything I can do — '

'There is,' said the inspector. 'I'm rather curious to know how you got into that cupboard. Suppose you tell us?'

Grasset turned to him. 'Well, sir, I'm afraid there is not much I can tell you. It all happened so suddenly.'

'Of course,' agreed the inspector. 'But how long were you in there? Have you any idea?'

Grasset glanced at the clock on the mantelpiece. 'I couldn't say for certain, but — ' He calculated. ' — I don't suppose it could have been more than forty-five minutes at the most.'

Mr. Drizzle nodded, and the butler continued. 'It is very difficult to know where to start,' he said slowly, 'so perhaps it would be as well if I told you *all* that happened this evening. I mean, it may not be important, but at least it will give you some idea of the order in which things occurred.'

He paused, as if trying to arrange his thoughts in sequence, then launched into a rather jagged account of the events of the last couple of hours.

'Ann, Mrs. Mimms and Mary went out at six,' he began. 'They said they wouldn't be back before ten, so I built up the kitchen fire and settled down to read. I had been at it for about half an hour when I heard someone on the stairs. Knowing that Mr. Trevelyn was in bed, and Miss Margery and the staff were out of the house, I wondered who it could be. I went through and found Mr. Trevelyn standing in the hall. He was just as surprised to see me I was to see him — more so, in fact. He asked me — you'll pardon me, sir, but these were his actual words — he asked me why the devil I wasn't with the others. Of course, I told him. I explained that I hadn't been feeling too well, so I had decided to remain indoors. I said I was sorry if I had startled him, and I asked him if there was anything he required. He shook his head and said there was not, but he was going to his study and on no account did he want to be disturbed. He said he was expecting a visitor, but I was not to bother listening for him as he would admit him himself. After that he went into the room and closed the door behind him. That was the last I saw of him.'

Grasset paused and Mr. Drizzle nodded.

'You say he was surprised to see you?'

'Very surprised, sir. Naturally he thought I'd gone to the fair with the others.'

'Would you say, then, that he was annoyed?'

'Yes — yes, I should say he was.'

'I see. Then it's possible that he gave you all the evening off so that he could have the house to himself.'

Grasset hesitated, but before he had time to reply Margery broke in.

'That's absurd,' she said sharply. 'Why on earth should he want to do that?'

'He was expecting a visitor,' reminded Mr. Drizzle gently.

'He's had visitors before,' she argued, 'but that's no reason why he should want to get rid of everybody. And anyway, he must have known I should turn up sooner or later.'

'Yes,' admitted Mr. Drizzle. He nodded and stroked his chin reflectively. 'Yes, that's perfectly true. However, we'll let that pass for the moment. Carry on, Grasset.'

The butler resumed his narrative.

'After Mr. Trevelyn had gone into the

study, I went back into the kitchen and settled once more into my book. I think I must have dozed, for I woke up with a start and felt something damp being pressed over my nose. It smelt horrid and sickly . . . '

'Chloroform,' muttered the inspector.

' . . . and although I struggled, I felt myself getting weaker and weaker, until at last everything went black. The next thing I knew, I was in the cupboard — though I wasn't aware of that till later. I tried to sit up, but I found that I couldn't, so I tried to call out, but that was impossible also. It wasn't until I felt the newspapers on which I lay that I guessed where I was. It occurred to me then that I might possibly be able to attract attention by kicking at the door — though I confess I hadn't much hope, as my feet were bound, too, and I had great difficulty in moving them. Anyway, I tried, and you have no idea how thankful I was when I heard someone turning the key.'

'I bet you were,' remarked Mr. Drizzle. 'And that's all you can tell us, is it? You didn't catch a glimpse of your attacker?'

The butler shook his head. 'I'm afraid not, sir.'

'Pity,' murmured the detective regretfully. 'Then you won't know how many there were?'

'No, sir. I didn't exactly see anybody, you know. I only felt them, as it were.' The butler lifted a shaky hand to his forehead and supported himself against the table. 'If you'll excuse me, miss,' he said, addressing Margery, 'I'll go and take a couple of aspirins. My head feels awful.'

'You're lucky you can feel it at all,' declared Mr. Drizzle. 'After a dose of that stuff, you shouldn't be able to tell you have a head.'

While Grasset went to his room, Margery and the inspector made a casual inspection of the kitchen. There was much evidence to support Grasset's story; a large, comfortable basket chair before the now dying fire and two cushions lying crumpled on the floor being the most corroborative. Close beside them was a book, and the carpet that was spread before the hearth was ruffled and curled. The inspection was purely methodical — on the inspector's part at least — and if Mr. Drizzle found anything worthy of special notice, he kept it entirely to himself.

A few minutes later, Grasset returned and declared, upon a concerned inquiry from Margery, that he felt a little better, though he was still looking decidedly pale. There were, however, two faint spots of crimson appearing on his cheeks, and Mr. Drizzle wondered how much of these were due to the whisky he had just taken.

'It's just struck me, sir,' said Grasset. 'You've telephoned for the police, I suppose?'

'We've tried,' corrected the little man with great stress on the last word, 'but the instrument isn't working.'

The butler raised his eyebrows in surprise. 'Not working? That's very strange. Perhaps — perhaps there's a line down,' he suggested helpfully.

'Perhaps,' agreed the inspector without much enthusiasm. 'Though I think we'll find it's only a cut wire somewhere. I'm afraid there's nothing for it but to drive down to the village in the car.' He glanced over at Margery. 'If you'll be all right — '

She nodded. 'I shall be,' she assured him firmly. 'As long as I know you're getting the police here, I don't mind.'

'Then in that case, I'd better be off,' said Mr. Drizzle. They went back to the drawing room from where the inspector collected his hat and coat, then once more came into the hall. 'You're sure?'

'Perfectly. Besides, I've got Grasset.' She opened the door for him. 'But you won't be long, will you?'

'I won't.' He gave her arm a gentle squeeze of assurance. 'I'll be back as quick as this bus can carry me. Goodbye.'

A few seconds later, the headlights of Mr. Drizzle's Bentley flashed down the drive and vanished into the darkness beyond.

4

Concerning a Silk Scarf

The doctor, his examination completed, rose to his feet and addressed the little group that was clustered round the inert figure of Matthew Trevelyn.

'I won't bother you with a lot of medical jargon,' he said as he removed his spectacles and walked over to his bag that lay on the desk. 'But in plain, common or garden English, he's been strangled.'

Sergeant Ansell of the Enderby police moved his somewhat cumbersome bulk nearer the body and stared down at it meditatively. 'I see,' he muttered. 'And you think there's no chance of suicide, eh?'

The doctor shook his head. 'Not the least,' he replied, shutting his bag with a snap. 'I agree with this gentleman here.' He nodded across to Mr. Drizzle. 'The scarf has been pulled tightly from the

41

back of the neck, and therefore it's impossible to suppose he committed suicide. No, Sergeant, you've got a job on this time. It's murder right enough.'

Whereupon Sergeant Ansell grunted; an officious sort of grunt that intimated he was not pleased. 'How long would you say he'd been dead, then?'

'Oh, let's see.' The doctor glanced speculatively at his watch. 'It's now ten minutes past nine. As near as I can tell you, about an hour and a half.'

Mr. Drizzle nodded and detached himself from the two policemen with whom he had been standing. 'Which would,' he remarked, 'put the murder at approximately half-past seven — half an hour before I arrived, wouldn't it?'

'That's it,' agreed the doctor. 'Well, I've done my bit, so you won't be wanting me anymore. I'll be able to give you a better report after the post-mortem, tomorrow morning.' He snatched up his bag and made for the door. 'If you've sent down for the ambulance, it should be here any minute. Anyway, I'll just have a look at Miss Trevelyn, then be off. See you tomorrow, Ansell. Good night, every-body.'

There was a chorus of muttered good nights, and the doctor left the study.

'Decent chap, Westwood,' commented Ansell. 'But I wish he wouldn't take things like this in such a damned matter-of-fact way. Now, sir.' He turned briskly to Mr. Drizzle. 'Perhaps you'll be able to give me a little more detail. There wasn't much time when you dragged us from the station, you know. You say you're from Scotland Yard?'

'That's right.' The other fished in his pocket for his warrant-card, found it, and handed it to the sergeant. 'My name's Drizzle — Detective Inspector Drizzle.'

'And you said you were visiting Mr. Trevelyn, I believe. Is that correct?'

'Perfectly. And in case you're wondering why on earth I should be visiting people at this time of night,' added the inspector, 'I'd better tell you that I had a breakdown on the road. But for that I should have landed here hours ago.' The stocky man sighed. 'I wish I had. I might have prevented this.'

Ansell looked at him sharply. 'What do you mean? Did you know anything — '

'About this? No, not really.'

'Then what was your reason for visiting Mr. Trevelyn? I don't want to pry into your personal affairs, you know, but in a case like this — ' He broke off impressively and left the remainder to Mr. Drizzle's imagination. 'Were you a friend of his?'

'Friend? Oh no.' The Scotland Yard man shook his head. 'No, I don't think you could call me a friend. I only met him once.'

'Then — '

'Perhaps I'd better explain,' went on the short man evenly. 'I'm here merely in response to a letter I received this morning. It was a rather peculiar letter, and I hardly knew what to make of it. In the course of a week we receive dozens of this sort at Scotland Yard, you know, but generally speaking we don't attach much importance to them. It's very seldom they mean anything. This one, however, struck me as being rather different. You see, as I've just said, I only met Mr. Trevelyn once, and that must have been over six years ago. It was only a casual meeting — some dinner, I believe — and until this morning I'd forgotten there was such a person. Apparently he hadn't forgotten me, however, and I was rather curious to know why. There wasn't anything important claiming my attention at the moment, so I decided to look into it myself. Strictly speaking, I should have informed you people before I came down here, but — well, as I didn't really believe there would be much in it, I didn't bother.' He suddenly produced an envelope and extracted from it a sheet of expensive-looking notepaper. 'This is the letter. Perhaps you'd like to see it. Rather interesting, don't you think? Especially after what's happened now.'

Ansell took the letter and read it curiously. It was short and cryptic — so cryptic that unless Ansell had been aware of its genuineness, he would have sworn it had come out of some seven-and-sixpenny thriller. It ran simply as follows:

Friar's Lodge,
Enderby,

Surrey.
September 12th, 19 —

Dear Inspector Drizzle,

I need your help. Why, I'm afraid I cannot write in this letter, nor can I explain over the telephone. All I *can* say is that my trouble justifies your assistance. I ask you, therefore, to come to see me tomorrow — the 13th — as soon as you can. Everything depends on whether you come — perhaps even my life. If you want to help me, for God's sake come — but it must be tomorrow.

Earnestly yours,
Matthew Trevelyn.

'Humph!' grunted Ansell. He handed back the letter. 'If he knew his life was in danger, why on earth didn't he come to us?'

'Perhaps he only *thought* it was,' replied Mr. Drizzle. 'In which case he would probably be too scared to confide in anyone locally. He became thoughtful.

'All the same, I'd like to know who the other visitor was he was expecting tonight.'

'Other visitor?' Ansell stared. 'Was he expecting somebody else besides you?'

Mr. Drizzle nodded. 'According to Grasset — he's the butler, you know — Mr. Trevelyn got out of bed for the purpose of receiving this visitor. Whether he was responsible for this job, I wouldn't like to say.'

'Who was he? Does Grasset know?'

'I don't think so. Neither does Miss Trevelyn.'

'Mm.' The sergeant put his notebook away. 'I'd like to have a word with this butler afterwards. You don't think he did it, do you?'

'Grasset?' Mr. Drizzle laughed. 'How could he? We found him in the cupboard trussed up like a chicken.'

'All the same,' insisted Ansell, 'he was the only one in the house at the time of the crime.' He picked up the silk scarf which the doctor had placed on the table and turned to the constables. 'We'll leave you to it now, Thorne. I don't suppose you'll find much more. You'll let me know when the ambulance arrives, won't you? I'm going to have a word with Miss Trevelyn.'

The policemen nodded, and began to complete their routine work as Mr. Drizzle and the sergeant left the study.

They met Grasset at the foot of the stairs. 'Just the man I want,' said Ansell. 'We're leaving Mr. Trevelyn in the study until the ambulance arrives. There are two of my men with him, but if the other servants arrive before we get him away, you'll see they don't go in, won't you?'

Grasset nodded. 'Of course, sir. I'll tell them. They shouldn't be very long. Perhaps — ' He broke off as he caught sight of the remnant of silk in the sergeant's hand. 'Why — why, that's Miss Trevelyn's scarf, sir. Wherever did you find it?'

'Eh?' Ansell looked with surprise at the object in question. 'Oh, this? Where did you expect we found it? Round Mr. Trevelyn's neck, of course. It was what he was strangled with.'

Grasset eyed him in astonishment. 'But — but that's impossible. Why, the scarf's been missing — '

'Missing?' It was Mr. Drizzle who spoke.

'Well . . . ' Grasset corrected himself somewhat. 'Not exactly missing. It hasn't been in the house, I mean. Miss Trevelyn said she left it at Mr. Manton's a few days ago.'

'She did, did she? Then how do you account for it being here?'

'I really couldn't say, sir. Unless it was brought by — ' Grasset broke off as he realized the strong implication in his words. 'No, it couldn't be that. Mr. Manton would never — '

'Would never kill Mr. Trevelyn? Is that that you were going to say? What makes you so sure?'

Grasset hesitated. 'Because he isn't that sort of gentleman, sir. He may be a little hot-tempered at times, but . . . Besides, what reason could he have?'

'Judging by the incident between him and Mr. Trevelyn last night,' said Mr. Drizzle, 'I should say that he had every reason. Rather a disturbance then, wasn't there?'

'Last night?' Grasset was surprised. 'How — how did you know?'

'Gossip travels pretty quickly in a village. I got it as I passed through.'

'Yes, I heard a bit about that, too,' put in Ansell, not to be outdone in the knowledge of local affairs. 'A rare how-d'you-do, wasn't there? At least, some of the lads in the village were saying.'

'That,' protested Grasset, icily, 'can hardly have anything to do with this. I'm sure Mr. Manton never meant what he said. It was only in the heat of the moment — '

'That depends on what he said,' broke in Mr. Drizzle. 'Suppose you tell us?'

Grasset seemed reluctant. 'I don't want to say anything against Mr. Manton. I don't believe for a moment that he . . . '

Ansell nodded, and after a little persuasion — for the butler seemed determined not to incriminate the popular Mr. Manton — the two detectives gained possession of the facts as far as he knew them. From what the servants had heard — and really, declared Grasset, one could hardly help hearing — Mr. Manton had kept his temper remarkably well. Mr. Trevelyn had been particularly insulting — though why, Grasset failed to understand, for the young writer was one of the nicest gentlemen he had ever met. But it was not until Mr. Trevelyn had threatened to have him thrown out that he became really angry.

'I think that's what did it, sir,' said Grasset with a shake of his head. 'Mr. Manton became terribly violent. Both Miss Trevelyn and I tried to pacify him, but I'm afraid it was no good.'

Ansell nodded. 'Did he make any threats against Mr. Trevelyn's life?'

'I'm afraid he did, sir, though I'm sure he didn't mean — '

'Can you remember what he said?'

The butler pondered. 'I can't remember everything, of course, sir. But there's one thing I do remember. He was just saying it as I entered the room after Mr. Trevelyn had rung for me. He was near the door at the time, and he said: 'I don't know what the hell you've got against me, but one of these days I'll choke the life out of you for what you've said — and that day isn't far off, either!'

'And the next day Mr. Trevelyn is strangled, eh? M'm!' Ansell mused. 'That sounds pretty bad for Mr. Manton. I should never have thought he was a man like that — though you never can tell with these writer chaps. They're so damned temperamental that they blow off steam at the slightest provocation.'

Mr. Drizzle made no comment. He was thinking. Was it possible that this young author was responsible for the crime? This was twice during the evening that his name had cropped up, and the occurrence could hardly be put down to coincidence. According to Mr. Balmer, the loquacious landlord of the Barrel Inn, the young man had wanted to marry Miss Trevelyn, but her uncle had refused to give permission. Could it be possible that the old man had been murdered solely to get him out of the way? It seemed absurd, yet Mr. Drizzle remembered hosts of other crimes in which the motive had been just as trivial. He sighed. This Mr. Manton was going to be quite an interesting person to meet — and Mr. Drizzle entertained not the slightest doubt that he would meet him.

With an emphatic reiteration of his belief in Mr. Manton's innocence, Grasset left them. Sergeant Ansell scratched his head and looked sideways at Mr. Drizzle.

'If you ask me, it's all over bar shouting,' he grunted. 'Looks as though young Manton's the man. He seems to have every motive — and, don't forget, he's a writer.'

He uttered the last words in a tone that clearly implied his opinion that gentlemen of the literary profession were capable of anything. Mr. Drizzle smiled.

'Don't you think it's a bit early to say that? Of course, I haven't met the gentleman, I know but that isn't to say that because he writes crime stories he's a murderer.' From the expression on his face, Ansell seemed to doubt the matter. Mr. Drizzle continued, 'All the same, it will be interesting to find out where he was this evening at about half-past seven. But hadn't we better see the young lady?'

Ansell signified his agreement with a nod. They found Margery alone in the drawing-room, and she rose from her seat by the fireplace and turned to meet them as they entered. Red patches under her eyes and the evidence of a dampened handkerchief told them she had been crying, but even the sorrow and worry through which she was passing failed to spoil the beauty of her small oval face; if anything, it seemed to accentuate it. Mr. Drizzle marvelled at the wonderful way in which she was keeping up.

'We don't want to bother you very much now, Miss Trevelyn,' he said, 'but I think Sergeant Ansell would like to ask you a few questions, if you don't mind.'

The sergeant slipped the scarf on the table and put his cap on top of it. He then stepped forward and produced his note-book and pencil — an impressive procedure that was done more to cover up his discomfiture than anything else, for it was quite evident from his manner that he wasn't enjoying himself in the least. Mr. Drizzle, on the other hand, had been on too many such cases to be affected.

'Now, Miss Trevelyn,' said Ansell after opening his mouth once or twice in a vain attempt to begin, 'as you know, in a job like this, it's our business to catch the person or persons responsible. To do that, however, we must ask everybody concerned all sorts of questions — many of which we don't like. So if I ask you something you feel is rather personal, I don't want you to feel embarrassed or annoyed; I want you to answer me as clearly as you can.' She nodded.

'I quite understand.'

'Thank you.' Ansell felt that he had broken the ice nicely. 'Now, you must be aware, I think, that there is some rather unpleasant talk going around the village. You mustn't blame your servants; they will talk. I am referring, of course, to the quarrel between your uncle and Mr. Manton of Briar Cottage, which occurred last night. What was that quarrel about?'

She looked at him in surprise. 'Is that question necessary?'

'I'm afraid so.'

'Very well.' She lowered her head and toyed with the small square of cambric that was screwed between her fingers. A gentle flush stole into her cheeks. 'The quarrel was about me. You see, Phillip — Mr. Manton — and I have been friends ever since he came to Enderby, and from that time he's been quite a frequent visitor to this house. A few days ago he asked me to marry him. I accepted, and last night it was decided that we should obtain my uncle's permission.'

Ansell nodded. 'And did you expect any difficulty in that direction, then?'

Margery shook her head. 'Of course not. Uncle and Phillip were quite friendly. We both thought it would be easy. But — but I'm afraid it wasn't. We never dreamed of anything like that.' She paused, and a frown of perplexity creased her brow. 'I couldn't understand it. Uncle had no reason whatever to turn against Phillip — at least, no real reason. And anyway, whatever he thought, there was no need for him to be so insulting. I've never known him like that before. He spoke to Phillip as if he . . . loathed him.'

'I see.' Ansell coughed. 'And what was the reason for your uncle's opposition?'

She shook her head. 'I don't know. Some absurd objection to Phillip's profession, I believe. Up to then, Uncle had been rather interested in Phillip's work — he's a writer, you know — but last night he seemed to have changed completely. He said something about him not wanting me to be married to a man who had to rely on a pen for a living, and — oh, and hosts of other ridiculous reasons. Anyone would have thought it was something low and degrading to be married to a writer.'

'Perhaps his hatred was directed more to Mr. Manton himself than his profession,' suggested Mr. Drizzle.

'I don't see — '

'I mean,' explained the Scotland Yard man slowly, 'perhaps all that about him not wanting you to marry an author was simply an excuse, the real reason being a sudden hatred towards Mr. Manton personally.'

She remained silent for a moment, obviously contemplating the possibility. Then: 'I don't know. Why should he have hated Phillip? Until yesterday, they were quite friendly.'

Mr. Drizzle nodded and the sergeant

continued. 'You said a few minutes ago,' he remarked, referring to his notebook, 'that Mr. Manton was a frequent visitor to this house. Mr. Manton rents a small place known as Briar Cottage, I believe. Did you ever go there?'

'Oh yes,' she answered without hesitation. 'Often.'

'Very well. Now, Miss Trevelyn, I want you to think carefully, because the next question is important. Did you ever leave your scarf at Mr. Manton's?'

'My scarf?' Margery regarded him in some surprise. 'Yes, I believe I did. Why do you ask?'

Ansell moved to the table. He lifted his cap and drew from underneath it the small length of silk. 'Is this yours, miss?'

She gave it but a glance, and her recognition was obvious. 'Yes — yes, of course, it's mine. But why — ' She broke off with a gasp as she suddenly realized his meaning. 'You don't think — '

'This is the scarf by which your uncle was murdered, Miss Trevelyn. You recognize it as belonging to you. And by your own admission, you say you left it at Mr.

Manton's during a visit there. How, then,' said Ansell, and there was a perceptible change in his voice, 'does it come to be here?'

5

Mr. Drizzle Decides to Stay

Margery stood motionless for a moment, white-faced and trembling. A grey mist swam before her eyes, and she clutched unsteadily at the mantelpiece. There was no mistaking the dreadful meaning that lay behind the sergeant's quietly spoken words. Quite obviously he thought that Phillip . . . but no; she shut the thought from her mind. That was impossible. It was an idea too dreadful even to contemplate. Yet . . . She became conscious that both men were staring at her expectantly and with an effort she forced herself to think clearly.

'I'm afraid, Sergeant Ansell, you're making a ridiculous mistake,' she said, and she was surprised at the iciness of her tone. 'Most certainly I left my scarf at Mr. Manton's — I'm frightfully careless that way — but you don't seem to regard the possibility of me calling for it again.'

'You mean — ?' Ansell was surprised.

She nodded. 'Of course. I brought it back myself yesterday.' The sergeant grunted. This fresh point of which he had never even thought made quite a hole in his theory, and he wasn't pleased.

'Anyway,' he said, 'how do you account for it being in the study? Perhaps you can tell me that?'

She shook her head. 'I'm afraid I can't. No doubt I left it there myself. I've a nasty habit of leaving things lying about.' She laughed — a shaky, forced little sound. 'I'm sorry to disappoint you, Sergeant, but if you're trying to pin this onto Mr. Manton — well, you're mistaken, that's all. Phillip left this house last evening and hasn't been back since. I can prove that.'

'Perhaps,' interposed Mr. Drizzle, gently, 'Miss Trevelyn would be good enough to do so.' He turned to her. 'I believe you stated earlier this evening that you had been with a friend all day. That friend was Mr. Manton, I presume?'

'Certainly. I left home in the middle of the morning and have been with him ever since. We had lunch and tea together at his cottage.'

'And what time did you leave him?'

'About a quarter-past seven, I believe. Yes, it would be a quarter-past seven, because I wanted to get down to Mr. Gregg's shop before it closed at half-past.'

'I see. And what did you do after you left him?'

'I went into the village, got what I wanted, and walked slowly back again.'

'And you got in at — ?'

'Not many minutes before you arrived. Just before eight, it would be.'

Ansell dropped the scarf on the table and turned to her with a certain amount of triumph in his movement. 'Then it's not impossible for Mr. Manton to have come here while you were in the village, is it?'

Mr. Drizzle cut short Margery's hot reply with a shake of his head. 'Unless he's capable of being in two places at once, I'm afraid it is, Ansell.'

The sergeant looked at the little man sharply. 'What do you mean?' he asked, more puzzled than anything else.

'Because at approximately twenty minutes to eight I saw him. I dropped into the Barrel before I came up here — driving makes you thirsty, you know — and I happened to see him as he went out.' The Scotland Yard man smiled at the sergeant's dazed expression. 'I put it like this: If Mr. Manton committed the murder, he would have had to leave his cottage immediately after Miss Trevelyn had gone. I don't know where he lives, but allowing him at least five minutes to get here, he would have to commit the murder, attend to Grasset, cut the telephone wire in some obscure corner, and get down to the Barrel by half-past. No, Ansell, unless he has the power of wings, I don't think it's possible.'

Margery gave an audible sigh of relief and shot him a glance of gratitude. Ansell, however, was not at all satisfied.

'That's all very well,' he said. 'But how do you know it was Manton? I thought you said you hadn't met him?'

'That's perfectly correct; I haven't,' conceded Mr. Drizzle. 'But the gentleman who served me happened to mention his name. I didn't actually see his face, but

I'm sure if you go down to the Barrel and see the person who served me — he's quite a talkative gentleman, by the way — he'll tell you.'

'Oh, well.' Ansell shrugged resignedly. 'That seems to let him out.' He glanced across at Margery. 'I'm very sorry, Miss Trevelyn, but I'm sure you'll see how bad things looked against Mr. Manton, especially after the things he said last night. However, I'll have a word with him myself tomorrow.' He closed his notebook with a snap that suggested that the interrogation was over, for the time being at any rate. 'I don't mind telling you, Miss Trevelyn, it looked pretty grim for Mr. Manton until Inspector Drizzle spoke up. However — '

That was as far as he got, for, as he turned to reach for his cap, his conversation was interrupted by a loud yell. Ansell looked quickly at Mr. Drizzle.

'What the deuce — ?'

Another cry, fainter this time, came from the direction of the study, followed almost immediately by the sound of smashing glass. Mr. Drizzle was across the room in a second, and out into the hall before either of them realized he had gone.

The door of the study was open when he reached it, and a strong draught was blowing through the open French windows, in one half of which was a large jagged hole. Negotiating the still figure of Matthew Trevelyn, he dashed to the window and narrowly missed another figure that was sprawled on the terrace.

'He's there!' shouted one of the policemen as he ran up to Mr. Drizzle's elbow. 'Over yonder!'

The moon, which for the past couple of hours had been struggling fitfully through a heavy sky of beleaguering clouds, was now completely obscured, and the night was intensely dark. But from the light of the study, the inspector was just able to make out the dim lines of a shadowy figure fleeing across the smooth carpet of lawn. In a second, Mr. Drizzle was off, dodging swiftly between the row of shrubs that bordered the green and cutting after the running figure as fast as his short legs would carry him.

The chase didn't last long. His quarry in front of him suddenly disappeared among a patch of trees, the large coat in which he was clad flowing loosely behind him. Panting madly, the stocky man flew after him — until a crash that shook every bone in his body halted his pace, and with a gasp he rolled over on the turf. Feeling very much as if a stone wall had hit him, Mr. Drizzle sat up — and realized with a start that he had run squarely into a tree. With language expressive of the occasion, he scrambled to his feet and dazedly surveyed the darkness around him. There wasn't a sound, save for the soft whine of the wind in the trees. The marauder was gone.

It was no use continuing the pursuit. By now the man might have gone in any one of a dozen different directions, and Mr. Drizzle was not disposed to search the whole neighbourhood. Mentally cursing his ill luck, he staggered unsteadily back to the house. He was met first on the terrace by Sergeant Ansell.

'Did you find him?'

Mr. Drizzle, his temper as well as his

person considerably ruffled, regarded the sergeant with a glare that should have withered him on the spot.

'No. But there's one thing I did find,' he said as he fingered his nose tenderly. 'I found out what it's like to be a battering ram. I never knew the bark of a tree could be so confoundedly hard.'

Ansell disappointedly, without the least concern for Mr. Drizzle's personal injuries. 'Did you see who it was?'

'Not having the eyes of a cat,' replied the stocky man testily, 'I'm afraid I didn't. What's it all about, anyway? Does anybody — Hullo!'

He broke off with an exclamation as he caught sight of Grasset, who, with a large white handkerchief, was dabbing an angry-looking wound on his forehead. 'What's happened to you? You didn't get in the way of a tree, did you?'

Grasset smiled faintly. 'No, sir. It was the — um — gentleman on the terrace.'

'What gentleman?'

'The one you've been sprinting after,' explained Ansell. 'Grasset found him looking through the window. He ran away when he heard someone coming, but Grasset yelled after him. Before he caught up with him, however, the chap picked up a plant pot that happened to have been left on the terrace and slung it at him. Hit Grasset a nasty whack on the head, it did, then went clean through the window. That was the crash we heard.'

'M'm!' Mr. Drizzle nodded sympathetically to the butler. 'You seem to be clean out of luck tonight. Do you know who it was?'

'I'm afraid not, sir,' replied Grasset with a shake of his head. 'He didn't let me get near enough to recognize him. But I did see him drop something as he ran away.' He scanned the paved terrace intently. 'Came out of his pocket, I believe. Something white.'

'What was it? A handkerchief?'

'No, sir. A piece of paper, I think. Yes, I'm certain it was. Ah, here it is.'

He stooped under one of the shrubs and picked up from underneath it a small scrap of paper. He looked at it curiously, turned it over once or twice, then handed it to Mr. Drizzle.

'Nothing very much after all, sir. Looks like the corner of a postcard.'

Mr. Drizzle walked over to the window and examined it in the light of the study. 'You're sure this is what fell from his pocket?'

'Oh, perfectly, sir,' said Grasset with conviction. 'I saw it quite plainly as he ran away. I don't suppose it'll be much good, though.'

Mr. Drizzle didn't reply. He handed it to the sergeant. 'What do you make of it?'

Ansell inspected without much enthusiasm. It was a small triangular piece of pasteboard, obviously torn from a postcard. On one side was a penny stamp, heavily obliterated by a smudgy postmark, and on the other, in black printed characters, were the letters: 'HARM . . . ' The rest of the word was missing. Ansell grunted.

'Not much. I don't see what good it is.'

'You don't?' Mr. Drizzle smiled. 'I think it may prove quite a useful clue to the identity of our unknown visitor.'

'Eh?' Ansell looked at him in surprise. 'How do you make that out? Why, even the address is missing.'

'You want too much for your money,' declared Mr. Drizzle dryly. 'It would have been easier if the address had been there, certainly. All the same, I think it may prove useful despite that.'

'Then I wish you'd tell me how,' said Sergeant Ansell irritably. 'Personally, I think — '

'If you look at the postmark,' interrupted Mr. Drizzle quietly, 'you'll see that the card was posted in Helmthorpe at approximately ten-fifteen yesterday morning.'

'Yes, I noticed that,' said Ansell, who had done nothing of the sort. 'But — '

'Look at the card itself, and you'll see that it's not an ordinary postcard like the ones you can buy at any stationer's shop. It is one of those specially printed sort used in business. That being so, I expect quite a few of them will pass through the post office at one time or another. If I were you, I should send it to the postmaster over at Helmthorpe and ask him if he recognizes it from what little print there is showing. If he does, he should be able to

70

tell you the name of the people it came from, and in that case — well, there you are.'

'Ye-es,' said Ansell slowly. Mr. Drizzle's idea began to impress him and he rubbed his chin reflectively. 'Yes, you're right. If we could find out where it came from in the first place . . . It's not much to go on, but there's a chance.' He took out his notebook and stowed the fragment carefully inside. 'Thank you very much, sir. I'll see to that the first thing in the morning.'

Any further conversation was interrupted by the arrival of the ambulance. Two powerful headlights flashed among the trees as it came up the drive. Sergeant Ansell dashed inside and prepared to conduct the removal of the body.

It didn't take long. Margery, tear-eyed and trembling, watched proceedings from the hall until Mr. Drizzle went up to her and placed a gentle hand on her shoulder. Without a murmur she allowed herself to be led quietly into the drawing room, and five minutes later Sergeant Ansell strode in to announce that it was all over.

'There's only the other servants to interview, then I've finished,' he remarked, unsuccessfully suppressing a prodigious yawn. 'Of course — ' He cast a sidelong glance at Mr. Drizzle. ' — there's no reason why that should detain you, sir. You'll want to get back to London, I suppose?'

'No, I don't think I shall.' Mr. Drizzle looked at his watch. 'Not at this time of night. I'll drive down to the Barrel and see if they can put me up there.'

Margery, who had been sitting listlessly in a chair, looked up with a start. 'No!' She sprang to her feet and placed a restraining hand on his arm. 'You mustn't go. You mustn't leave me.'

'But my dear young lady — '

'You can stay here.' Her grip tightened and she spoke quickly. 'I'll tell the servants to prepare a room for you when they come in. You mustn't leave me now.'

'But — '

'Please.' She looked at him, and the note of pleading that had crept into her voice was reflected in the depths of her eyes. 'Mr. Drizzle, I want you to stay

— for my sake. I just couldn't bear a night on my own just now. You will, won't you — ?'

He smiled and pressed her hand gently. 'If you want me to, I'll stay — and believe me, there's nothing I'd like better. I was hoping you'd ask me.'

She nodded and flopped back into the chair. 'Thank you,' she said softly.

And at that moment Grasset, his head now enveloped in a white bandage, tapped discreetly at the door, and announced wearily that the other servants had arrived.

6

The Searcher

Briar Cottage stood silent and dark. Not a sound broke the natural stillness of the evening, except the soft whine of the wind as it sighed round the picturesque gables and chimneys. Somewhere in the distance the church clock broke into two muffled chimes, then died away in a silence that seemed to constitute the very night itself. At this hour, Enderby and its inhabitants were wrapped in slumber; and even the village constable, whose arduous duty it was to patrol the straggling streets, yawned, and composed himself to what little of the night there was left.

Yet the figure who was standing among a welter of rose bushes in the tiny garden of Briar Cottage still waited. Three minutes, six minutes, nine minutes went by, but he stood silent and motionless. He maintained this position until the clock struck again, and only then did he move. He compared his luminous wristwatch with the usually erratic judgment of the village clock, and found that for once the latter was correct: dead on a quarter-past.

The man breathed deeply and glanced at the shadowy bulk of the cottage. Not a light showed anywhere. He had been standing here for well over an hour, and it seemed unlikely that Phillip Manton would be awake now. Yet to underestimate that fact would be fatal. He pondered, and two cold splashes on the back of his hand made him look upwards. The sky was as black as pitch, and he knew that before long there would be another downpour of rain. This decided him, and he determined to risk it.

He took from the pocket of his heavy overcoat a large black handkerchief, and with extreme care he proceeded to fasten it over the lower half of his face. Recognition was now impossible. He then drew on a pair of thin black gloves, and with a cat-like tread extricated himself from the thorny embrace of the bushes and moved silently across the lawn.

With the attitude of one who knows exactly what he is going to do, he made his way to one of the lower front windows. He switched on a torch, and in the white beam he examined the frame carefully. He felt no trepidation as far as the torch was concerned. Save for Phillip Manton, there was little danger of anyone seeing the light, for the cottage was well off the beaten track, and it was unlikely that there would be anyone on such a lonely road at this time of night.

His lips curved in a smile of satisfaction beneath his mask, and he produced from one of his pockets a small knife-like instrument. Windows of this type were not usually made for keeping out burglars, and this one was no exception. Working in a slightly diffused light, for he could only lay the torch on the sill, he fumbled in the region of the catch, and a few seconds later a gentle click announced that his mode of entrance was open before him.

He stood listening for a moment to ascertain whether the sound had been heard, but apparently it hadn't, for all remained silent.

Gently, and with infinite caution, he raised the lower sash. It moved noiselessly, and for this the intruder was fervently grateful. Leaning through the window, he picked up the torch and directed its ray downwards. Immediately below him was a large soft settee, and it was onto this that he stepped a few seconds later. The springs creaked slightly as he lowered his weight onto them; but not enough, he thought, to penetrate to the rooms above.

Stepping down onto the carpet, he moved silently forward, the white beam of the torch cutting the pitch-black darkness like a knife. It was easy to see, even in this state of semi-gloom, to what use this apartment was put. The plain walls lined with dwarf bookcases told him it was a study, and this fact was borne out by the litter of paper and a typewriter that occupied the desk in the centre.

It was to this that the intruder first gave his attention. Laying the torch on the desk, he examined the papers carefully, and gave a grunt as he saw the words 'Chapter 3' on one of the sheets. Of course, this sort of thing was only to be expected in the home of a writer. Here, apparently, were born the novels over which book reviewers went crazy and the general public paid seven-and-sixpence to read. He grunted.

The search on the top of the desk resulted in nothing, and he turned his attention next to the drawers. There were seven — three down each side and one long one at the top. Each, however, were filled with quantities of typing paper, carbon, and other such commodities of a writer, and it was easy to see that what he was looking for wasn't there.

He flashed his torch round the apartment again, and the light came finally to rest on a well-filled bookcase. Of course — the very place. Crossing the room, he dropped on his knees before it and ran the light across the backs of the books. Many of them were expensive first editions, and he guessed that they were complimentary copies presented to Phillip Manton by members of his own profession.

He regarded the bookcase thoughtfully.

There would be twenty or thirty volumes here, and what he was looking for might be in any of them. With a grunt, he picked out the first one and began to flick through the pages. There was nothing. Quickly he pulled out another and clumsily repeated the process. He was just getting into the way of it when he reached the last one and found that it contained exactly the same as the others — nothing.

By now his patience was beginning to wear thin. There were other bookcases, but his failure with this one had damped his enthusiasm, and it occurred to him that they weren't such likely places after all. Flashing the torch round the room again, he began to pry into fresh objects; and by the time he had searched everything that was capable of being searched, his net result was nothing.

He gave vent to a snort of mingled disgust and annoyance and stood irresolutely in the centre of the room. Obviously the thing he was looking for was not here, and he came to the conclusion that it must be in some other room. The question was, which? As he knew that there were six rooms to this cottage — and society dictated that no house of six rooms or under could be anything but a cottage — it was going to be difficult.

A sudden click behind him made him turn, and as he did so, the clock on the mantelpiece struck the half hour. The time was more advanced than he had expected, and he knew that he would have to be getting on. Crossing the room, he silently opened the door and passed into the shadowy hall. He opened the first door he came to, and, flashing the ray of the torch round quickly, he saw that it was the sitting-room. It didn't seem that there were many places in which Phillip Manton would hide anything here, but for his own interests he could not afford to overlook anywhere. Stepping inside, he closed the door and began a rapid search of the apartment. In the dim light it was difficult, and for all that he found, he might never have bothered.

Leaving the sitting-room in annoyance, he next went to the kitchen. Apart from the oven, the refrigerator and one or two other domestic fittings, there seemed small chance of there being a place in which to hide anything here. He was right. After a swift search, he found there was nothing.

He began suddenly to experience a curious feeling of panic. After all the time he had waited, was he going to be cheated? Was his vigil going to be for nothing? Or perhaps — he caught his breath at the idea — perhaps the thing he was looking for was not here at all. He had no concrete proof that it was. And yet . . . No, it was absurd. It *must* be here, somewhere.

Calling himself several varieties of a fool, he at last succeeded in calming his frayed nerves a little. There was only one thing for it: he must look upstairs. The risk was colossal. If Manton should wake . . . His fingers closed upon a hard bulk in his pocket, and its presence did much to restore his courage.

Coming to the decision that he must get on with the job as soon as he could, he returned to the hall. He ascended the stairs slowly, testing each step with his foot before he allowed his full weight to rest upon it. He arrived at the top without incident, and in the light of the torch surveyed the landing. The door nearest to him was open, and he could see without flashing the light inside that it was a box-room. Trunks, boxes, discarded pictures and other such junk met his gaze. Perhaps here . . .

Tiptoeing quietly across the carpeted landing, he entered the room. After all, in a place full of rubbish, anything could be hidden. Unfortunately, the thing he was looking for wasn't, and he knew within a few minutes that he had failed again.

His face twisted under a scowl of chagrin. Where *could* it be . . . ? Then suddenly he stood bolt upright and uttered an involuntary exclamation of surprise. What a fool! What an imbecile! Why on earth hadn't he thought of it before? The most likely place for the object to be was Phillip Manton's bedroom itself. That was only logic, and he cursed himself for not having thought of it sooner. He turned the idea over in his mind, and as he did so he became more and more convinced that he was right. He had searched practically the whole of the house without discovering anything, and it was ten to one that if the object was in the house at all — and he was quite convinced that it was — then the most likely place for it to be found was Phillip Manton's bedroom.

He stepped out onto the landing and flashed the torch on the other doors. Which one was Manton's? There was no means of telling, but he rather thought that the one opposite him would be it. Its room would overlook the front. Treading silently to the door, he placed his ear to the jamb and listened. Faintly from inside came the metallic tick of a clock; and then, to his straining ears, the soft, steady sound of peaceful breathing. This was it, all right. Switching off the torch, his hand found the knob, and he turned it carefully. Save for a gentle grating, it moved easily. Slowly he pushed open the door, and, after hesitating a few seconds, stepped into the complete blackness of the room.

Whether it was some instinctive premonition of approaching danger, or whether it was the effect of his troubled mind,

Phillip Manton never knew. All that he did know was that he suddenly found himself completely awake, staring out into a world of impregnable blackness. What had awakened him he could not tell, but every sense was alert and tingling. For a few seconds he remained quite still, listening to the sound of his own breathing, which seemed amplified a hundred times in the solid silence of the room. Desperately he racked his brain for some tangible reason for his sudden consciousness, but found none. Perhaps it was the affair of tonight that had preyed upon his mind. Or perhaps it was Margery. He listened, and strained every nerve to recapture the sound that had obtruded upon his thoughts. It came again — a faint, almost imperceptible rustle outside his door. He stiffened and was about to raise himself on one elbow when the knob on his door gave a slight squeak. He couldn't see a thing, but he sensed, rather than heard, that the door was gently opening. Someone — heaven knew who — was entering his room.

He made no sound; he lay completely

still, waiting for the intruder's next move. A soft rustle told him that the unknown was approaching his bed, and he decided that it was time he took a hand in the proceedings. Before he had time to move, however, a sudden dazzling beam cut the darkness, and he gasped involuntarily.

The figure turned, startled, and his two eyes glinted like fire in the subdued light. His arm raised upwards, and Phillip caught a glimpse of something white, then something that seemed to cut into his very brain, descended with a crushing force upon his head. The white blur dissolved into a million flashes of crimson before his eyes, and he felt himself falling into a well of blackness to which there seemed no end . . .

7

Mr. Drizzle is Puzzled

Breakfast the following morning was a quiet meal, Margery at one end of the table contenting herself with a small piece of dry toast, while Mr. Drizzle at the other end attacked a large plate of eggs and bacon with undisguised gusto. Truth to tell, Mr. Drizzle was thinking, and it was one of his beliefs that one could never think properly on an empty stomach.

He was pleased Margery had asked him to stay. There was something about this affair that interested him — not from a morbid point of view, but from a professional aspect. Why had Matthew Trevelyn lived such a quiet life, shunning society so much that the only visitors he had were a chosen few? And what had been the reason for his sudden hatred of Phillip Manton? Then there was that letter he had received. He had shown it to Margery, but except for being surprised, she could offer no explanation for it whatever. These were only a few of the interesting facts about the case, and Mr. Drizzle felt that the answers, once found, would go a very long way to solving the mystery of the old man's death.

The meal was served by Ann, a thin, miserable-looking woman who had the most annoying habit of flitting in and out of the room like a ghost. Every time she entered, she regarded Mr. Drizzle in awe, then went off to the domestic regions to confide to Mrs. Mimms that the gentleman who had come last night looked more like a retired tailor than a policeman — and ate more than a stoker!

Margery, however, seemed quite oblivious of these frequent interruptions on Ann's part. She ate her meal almost mechanically, and it was obvious to Mr. Drizzle that something of great importance was occupying her mind. He was shrewd enough to guess that he formed part of her thoughts, for once or twice she glanced over in his direction and opened her mouth as if to make some remark. But her state of indecisiveness was evident, for she always averted her gaze without so much as commenting upon the brilliance of the morning.

Breakfast was just over when Ann entered again, this time to inform Mr. Drizzle that 'a gen'leman 'ad called' to see him. Excusing himself to Margery, who replied with a preoccupied nod, the stocky man made his way to the drawing room into which his visitor had been shown, and evinced no surprise when he saw that it was Ansell.

'Good morning, Sergeant,' he greeted. 'Don't tell me you've traced that postcard already?'

'No sir.' Ansell, who had been sunning himself by the window, raised his bulk from the depths of an exceedingly comfortable armchair and moved over to meet the detective. 'I haven't sent that off yet.'

'Of course not.' The little man extended his hand and gripped the other's firmly. 'I didn't suppose you had.'

Mr. Drizzle regarded the sergeant curiously. From the expression on his face, it seemed that Ansell was displeased about something, and Mr. Drizzle wondered what it was. He didn't wonder long.

'I came up so soon,' said Ansell, 'because I knew I couldn't get you on the phone. I thought you'd better know.'

'Know what?' asked Mr. Drizzle, puzzled.

'I've been through to the chief constable this morning, and he thinks we ought to call in the Yard,' Ansell grunted disparagingly. 'What's put that bee into his bonnet, I don't know. He seems to think that because we haven't had a murder case here before, we shan't be able to manage it. Anyway, I happened to mention you were here, and he said he would phone through to Scotland Yard straight away. Seeing you've been in this business from the beginning, he'd like you to take it over.'

Mr. Drizzle raised his eyebrows. So that was the cause of the sergeant's irritation. 'That's very interesting. Colonel Wade doesn't believe in wasting time, does he?'

Ansell stared. 'Do you know him?'

'Oh yes.' The stocky man smiled. 'Colonel Wade and I are old friends. Went to college together.'

The sergeant uttered something that sounded remarkably like another grunt, and Mr. Drizzle hastily turned his smile into a little cough.

'As far as I can see,' observed Ansell gruffly, 'there's no reason why we should bother you at all.'

Mr. Drizzle sighed inaudibly. Ansell was inclined to be difficult; he could see that. Obviously the country sergeant resented the prospect of outside interference. To a certain extent, this attitude was natural, for no provincial officer liked to think that his case was being handed over to a London colleague lock, stock and barrel, as it were. Nevertheless, the Scotland Yard man saw that if he was going to work on this case — and it now seemed extremely likely — any antagonism between the sergeant and himself would make things decidedly difficult. Mr. Drizzle rubbed the side of his chin and looked at the other carefully.

'Of course, Sergeant. I understand your

point of view perfectly.' His lips parted in a pleasant smile. 'But I know Colonel Wade very well, and I'm sure he didn't mean you to take it like that. Why, you're as good as stating he thinks you inefficient.'

Ansell looked uncomfortable. 'Well, he didn't say — '

'Of course he didn't. That's rot. But he probably realized how difficult a murder case can be and thought you might like a little help.'

The sergeant grunted doubtfully. 'That may be. All the same, I think he might have let us have a shot at it. It would have meant quite a lot to me if I could have pulled this off on my own.'

'You needn't bother about that where I'm concerned,' assured Mr. Drizzle. 'I'll see you don't lose any credit that's due to you.'

The stout man brightened somewhat. 'Well . . . perhaps he's right. All the same . . . '

'Of course he's right,' asserted Mr. Drizzle confidently. 'Take it from me, these jobs aren't all beer and skittles — I know; I've had some — and I shall be only too pleased to help you in any way I can. I shall have to stay for the inquest, so I might as well lend a hand as not.'

Ansell shrugged resignedly, and from his manner seemed somewhat mollified. 'I thought I'd better let you know how things stood, that's all.' He picked up his cap and made for the door. 'Colonel Wade is coming over this morning, so I expect he'll want to see you.'

Mr. Drizzle nodded and opened the door for him. 'Yes, I suppose he will. Thanks for coming to tell me, Ansell. I'm extremely grateful to you.'

Ansell waved away his thanks and crossed the hall to the open front door. Bidding the Scotland Yard man good morning, he descended the steps and crunched down the drive, at the bottom of which Mr. Drizzle guessed he would have a car waiting. Congratulating himself upon brushing over that situation more or less peaceably, Mr. Drizzle went back to the breakfast-room.

Margery was standing by the window as he entered, watching the retreating figure of the visitor as he disappeared from view among the bushes. She turned quickly from the window.

'That was Sergeant Ansell, wasn't it?'

He nodded.

'What did he want? I mean . . . did he have any news?'

Mr. Drizzle smiled. 'It's a bit early for news, yet, isn't it? No, he merely called to tell me that the chief constable has decided to call in Scotland Yard. He wants me to work on the case.'

'You mean . . . ' She caught her breath and looked at him in surprise. 'You mean you'll — have to stay?'

He nodded. The tone of her voice echoed the expression of absolute dismay that was pictured on her face, and he looked at her curiously.

'It does, if you can put up with me.'

'Oh, of course.' She recovered her composure quickly. 'I didn't mean that. I — I want you to stay. It's just — just that I wondered what you were going to do, that's all.'

'Well, if you'd rather I went down to the Barrel — '

'Oh no,' she broke in hastily. 'I — I'm only too pleased to know that you're staying. I only hope you'll be able to get to the bottom of this — this horrible business. And now,' she broke the conversation, 'if you'll excuse me, there are some things I ought to see to.'

He nodded; and with a smile — rather forced, he thought — she passed out of the room. He stared after her as she crossed the hall, and a frown wrinkled his forehead.

'That's strange,' he muttered. 'Very strange.'

For he could still see the look of dismay that had been on her face, and it puzzled him. Last night she had been eager for him to stay — had implored him, in fact — but now she seemed to have changed completely. His presence was no longer desired, and she was afraid. Afraid of what?

He sighed.

There was a lot that was puzzling and strange about this case.

8

The Telephone Message

It was about half-past ten when Mr.
Drizzle eventually arrived at the police
station. Drawing his car to a standstill before
the grey stone cottage, which had been
converted for that exalted purpose by the
local council, he went inside and was immediately conducted into the presence of
Sergeant Ansell and the chief constable.

Colonel Wade, a big, pleasant-faced individual who looked more like a prosperous
farmer than an officer of the law, greeted
Mr. Drizzle with a genial smile and a
hearty handshake.

'Pleased to see you, Drizzle,' he
boomed. 'Pleased to see you. Haven't set
eyes on you for ages. You've met Ansell,
haven't you?'

Mr. Drizzle nodded and said that he had,
and the sergeant, acting with a politeness
he by no means felt, pushed forward a

chair and invited the Scotland Yard man to sit down. Mr. Drizzle thanked him and availed himself of the invitation.

'Now then,' said the colonel, folding his arms and leaning across Ansell's private desk, of which he seemed to have taken full possession, 'we don't want to waste any time, so I suggest we get down to business straight away.' He glanced at Mr. Drizzle. 'I've been through to the assistant commissioner at Scotland Yard this morning, and there is absolutely no objection to you staying as far as they are concerned. That is,' he added, 'if you *want* to stay.'

'Oh, I do,' said Mr. Drizzle. 'I'd like to very much — if Sergeant Ansell doesn't mind.'

'Of course he doesn't,' put in Colonel Wade, as though the very idea was impossible. 'We were talking it over when you came in and he thinks it's a splendid idea, don't you, Ansell?'

The sergeant regarded him with an expressive stare, then, realizing that any further protest would be so much wasted breath, gave an audible sigh of resignation and nodded in agreement.

'Good,' said the chief constable, picking up one of Ansell's pens and prodding the desk with it. 'That's settled, then. Now, I've heard all about this business from Ansell. Suppose you give me your views?'

Mr. Drizzle crossed his legs and made himself as comfortable as the extremely hard chair would allow.

'I'm afraid I don't hold any views at the present,' he remarked. 'All we know up to now is that last evening, Matthew Trevelyn was found strangled in his study. Who did it, or why it was done, is yet to be discovered.'

'M'm,' said the chief constable, wrinkling his forehead. 'That doesn't tally with Ansell's version. According to what he said a few minutes ago, he seems pretty certain that a young fellow named Manton had something to do with it.'

'I didn't exactly say that,' protested the sergeant, colouring slightly. 'All the same, I don't believe it's as easy to rule him out as you think.'

Mr. Drizzle turned his head. 'Why not?' he demanded in some surprise. 'I told you last night that unless Manton had the power of wings, he couldn't possibly have done it.'

'Agreed,' said Ansell. 'In the ordinary circumstances, no.' He smiled superciliously. 'But you seem to have forgotten the power of a motor-car.'

Mr. Drizzle stared. 'What do you mean? You don't think — '

'Last night,' said Ansell, leaning forward in his chair, 'I was quite convinced from what you said that Manton could have had nothing to do with it. But this morning I've been thinking, and I'm equally convinced that if he used a car, it's not so impossible after all.'

Sergeant Ansell watched the result of his statement with an inward feeling of satisfaction. Mr. Drizzle pondered for a few moments and gently rubbed his chin. Colonel Wade allowed his gaze to wander between the two of them, then, after a short silence, ventured to ask what it was all about. In the least possible number of words, Mr. Drizzle outlined the situation as he saw it, and the colonel nodded.

'I see what you mean,' he said. 'To

commit the murder in that short time would be next to impossible, even with a car. You're sure it was Manton you saw?'

'As sure as I can be without actually seeing him,' replied Mr. Drizzle, 'and even then I doubt whether I should be able to recognize him. I merely accepted the barman's word that it was Phillip Manton, and unless he was lying — and I don't see why he should — I had no reason to doubt it. At all events, it shouldn't be very difficult to find out.'

The chief constable rolled the pen up and down the blotting pad and nodded. 'No, I don't suppose it should. But what about the car? Has this fellow — what d'you call him, Manton? Has he got one?'

'I think so,' replied Ansell, 'though I can't say for certain. But if he has, I'm willing to bet my pension that he had it out last night — and not far from Friar's Lodge, either.'

He uttered the last sentence almost defiantly as he looked at Mr. Drizzle, but if he expected any opposition from the inspector he was disappointed. Mr. Drizzle fumbled in his pocket, produced his pipe and asked whether they minded, and on being informed by the chief constable that they didn't, proceeded to fill it with tobacco.

'I don't think we need quarrel over that,' he said as he struck a match. 'We shall be seeing Manton himself before long, so we'll soon get to know. What we have to look for first is the motive, and, though I admit Manton has one of a sort, I hardly think he'd risk the gallows for the sake of marrying Margery Trevelyn, attractive as that young lady undoubtedly is.'

Ansell grunted. 'You don't know what anyone'll do where a woman is concerned,' he said, and the chief constable smiled.

'Ansell's a confirmed bachelor,' he explained, 'and I believe he objects to all women on principle.'

How much of this somewhat slanderous statement was true, Mr. Drizzle had no means of telling, but nevertheless Ansell turned a very deep red, and was only saved the indignity of further remarks on the subject by the sudden clamour of the telephone bell. He snatched at the instrument gratefully and lifted the receiver to his ear.

'Hello . . . ? Yes, yes, this is the police station,' he said irritably. 'What did you say . . . ? You're who . . . ? Oh, Mrs. Gribbs, eh?' The look of annoyance on Ansell's fleshy face was suddenly replaced by one of intense interest, and he listened while the voice at the other end went on talking. 'What's that . . . ? You've had a *what*?' He shouted almost incredulously into the receiver. 'Yes, I heard you . . . All right, I'll be over . . . in a few minutes, yes . . . Good-bye.'

He returned the receiver to the hook and faced them quickly. 'If that doesn't beat the band, then I don't know what does!' he remarked forcibly. 'Do you know who that was? It was Mrs. Gribbs — she's the woman who goes and does for Mr. Manton, you know. And do you know what she wanted? She wanted someone to go over to Briar Cottage straight away.'

Ansell paused, probably with the intention of creating a minor suspense, but more probably from lack of breath.

'Well?' It was Colonel Wade who spoke, and he sounded irritated.

'Mr. Manton had a visitor last night,' continued the stout sergeant hastily. 'Someone broke into his cottage and attacked him while he was in bed. Mrs. Gribbs found him when she went to clean up.'

Mr. Drizzle started and snatched the pipe from his lips. 'What do you mean, 'found' him? You don't mean there's been *another* murder?'

'Not quite.' Ansell jumped to his feet and reached for his cap. 'But according to Mrs. Gribbs, it's a wonder there hasn't been.'

9

The Manuscript

In the daytime, Briar Cottage held pretensions to a beauty that one often sees on an artist's canvas, but seldom in actual fact. It stood literally in a sea of roses, and in the sharp morning sunlight the blooms drenched the air with a fragrance entirely of their own — ample testimony to the complete disregard of Nature to the sordid events of modern life. Sergeant Ansell and Mr. Drizzle could not help admiring the atmosphere of old-world charm that pervaded the place, as the Scotland Yard man's open tourer stopped before the gate.

'This,' said Mr. Drizzle, dreamily, 'is the sort of place I should like to have when I retire. Far from the madding crowd and all that sort of thing.'

The sergeant didn't answer, but climbed ponderously out of the car. Pushing open the small gate, they walked up the stone pathway and came to the porch-covered front door. Mr. Drizzle raised the knocker and gave two sharp taps, and the door was opened almost immediately by a tall, emaciated woman in a large coarse apron. This, apparently, was Mrs. Gribbs.

'Good morning, madam,' said Ansell, who took over proceedings automatically. 'We're here in response to the telephone message received at the police station a short while ago, and — '

Mrs. Gribbs terminated his flow of official jargon by clapping a bony hand to her chest in a wail of thankfulness.

'Thank 'eaven you've come,' she cried, motioning them to step inside. 'If it wasn't for poor Mr. Manton, I wouldn't stop in this 'ouse another minute — that I wouldn't. What the world is comin' to, I don't know. Scandalous it is, that's what I say. Scandalous!'

Ansell made no reply, not being able to think of one suitable at the moment; and as Mr. Drizzle seemed to be taking no part in the conversation at all, the woman decided that the best thing to do would be to present them to Mr. Manton. With a great display of ceremony, she conducted them to the study.

Phillip Manton was seated by the open window when they entered, a small bandage tied tightly round his head. He rose to his feet to meet them, and in the bright sunlight that flooded the room Mr. Drizzle was able to take a good look at him without appearing to do so.

The impression was favourable, and the stocky man decided that whatever objection Matthew Trevelyn had had to his niece's association with him, it could not have been his looks. He was a tall, lithe young man, somewhere between twenty-five and thirty, and his features, while not being exactly handsome, were distinctive of character. His clear blue eyes were large and sparkling, and in them was an expression of deep intelligence. To Mr. Drizzle, who was used to summing up his fellow creatures, he seemed to be one of those few people who possess that uncommon virtue, common sense.

Phillip smiled wanly and invited them to sit down. 'After what my housekeeper said on the telephone, you must have thought I was very nearly dead,' he remarked. 'I'm afraid I frightened Mrs. Gribbs so much that she hardly knew what she was saying.'

A muffled sniff outside the door intimated that Mrs. Gribbs agreed with him, and Sergeant Ansell nodded. 'I hardly expected to find you in the land of the living,' he confessed. 'Just what is this all about?'

Phillip, who seemed slightly puzzled at Mr. Drizzle's presence, began his narrative hesitatingly. 'I'm afraid I can't tell you that,' he answered. 'All I can say is that somebody broke into my cottage last night, searched the place from top to bottom, and finally came to my room. For some reason I can't understand, I awoke just as he was entering my room, and because I was foolish enough to acquaint him with that fact, he clubbed me.' He smiled ruefully. 'It's really very silly, you know. I've written about such situations dozens of times, but never actually experienced one. And now when I do, I go and put my foot in it like that!'

'M'm!' Ansell scratched his chin. 'You say he searched the house? What was he looking for? Have you any idea?'

'I'm afraid I haven't,' said Phillip with a shake of his head.

'Do you keep any valuables here?'

'Apart from my typewriter,' replied Phillip, nodding across to the desk, 'there's nothing of value in this house. Unless,' he added dryly, 'he's taken a fancy to my books and thought he'd like to read them in their home of origin.'

The sergeant grunted. 'Then there's nothing missing?'

'Not a thing — as far as I can see.'

'Seems pretty pointless to me. How did this fellow get in?'

'By the window, I believe.' Phillip glanced past them to where the curtains were swaying gently in the breeze. 'Mrs. Gribbs found it open when she came this morning. That was how she got in. I was out to the wide, then.'

Ansell rose to his feet and examined the ledge. Except for one or two scratches on the paintwork, there was nothing.

'We'll have a look outside in a few minutes,' he said as he turned back. 'Is there anything else you can tell us?'

'I'm afraid not,' said Phillip. 'You see — '

Mr. Drizzle broke in. 'You didn't recognize the intruder, then?'

'Good Lord, no!' exclaimed Phillip. 'I should have told you if I had.'

'But you saw *something* of him?'

'Well — ' Phillip frowned and hesitated. 'I suppose I did. But nothing by which I should know him again. It was only for a second when he put the light on. I could see just two things. A large black mask that covered the lower half of his face, and — somewhere about him, I can't say where — something very white. It might have been a scarf or it might have been my imagination. I don't know. I only saw it for a second.'

'I see,' said Mr. Drizzle with a nod. 'And did he search your room?'

'Judging by the various articles of underwear that are scattered over my bedroom floor, I should say he did,' said Phillip with emphasis.

'It was the only room in which he didn't attempt to leave things as he found them.'

'I trust you haven't touched anything,' said Ansell. 'Fingerprints, you know . . . '

The young author smiled. 'You needn't be afraid of that,' he said. 'You won't find I've touched anything important — or Mrs. Gribbs, either. I'm quite well educated in these matters.'

'Good,' said the sergeant with a nod. 'Then perhaps we'd better have a look outside now.'

Mr. Drizzle rose to his feet. 'Yes, I suppose we had,' he agreed, 'though I'm afraid it won't be any good.'

Ansell looked at him sharply. 'Why not?' he

'Because it rained cats and dogs last night,' replied the inspector.

'Of course.' Ansell grunted. 'I'd forgotten that. Anyway, we'd better have a look.'

Accompanied by the young writer, the two police officials went outside. The ground under the window was hard, stoned in the crazy paving style; and except for an upturned soap box upon which Mrs. Gribbs had apparently executed her gymnastic entrance, there was nothing. Whatever marks there might have been had been washed away by the rain of the previous evening.

A brief examination of the window from

the outside proved what Mr. Drizzle already guessed. The catch had been shot back by some steel instrument that must have been no thicker than a pen-knife, and there was nothing to be learned there. Nor did they find anything in the garden. The intruder seemed to have exited as unobtrusively as he had entered, and left no trace on either occasion. Ansell was displeased.

'We don't seem to be getting on very far, do we?' he commented. He shot a quick glance at Phillip. 'What about the garage?'

'The garage?'

'Yes. You have a car, haven't you?'

'Oh!' Phillip comprehended. 'Yes, I have a car, but surely you don't think he'd want to tamper with that?'

'Seeing from what you say that he has tampered with nearly everything in the house, I see no reason why he should make an exception of this. I'd like to have a look, anyway.'

Mr. Drizzle smiled gently. It was easy to see what Ansell was getting at. He was looking for something to support his car theory in the Trevelyn murder, and he apparently did not intend to leave without exploiting that theory.

The young man hesitated for a few seconds, as though he was reluctant to accede to the sergeant's request. Then, with a little nod, he led them round the side of the house to the back.

The garage was a wooden construction standing on a square of recently laid concrete, from which a broad gravel path led to a gate in the hedge. Apparently someone had been in recently, for the doors were unlocked; opening one of them, Phillip stood aside and allowed them to pass in.

The car, a cream-coloured Humber, stood in the centre and occupied quite a considerable portion of what little room there was. Despite the bright morning sunshine outside, the interior was gloomy, and Phillip switched on a light.

'Doesn't seem to have been anybody here,' commented Ansell.

'There hasn't. The place is just as I left it when I put the car in last night.'

'Last night? Did you have your car out then?'

'I — ' Phillip bit his lip, and it was

evident that he had said something he regretted.

'Yes I did. Only a short run. I was too tired to go far.'

'Yet you regained sufficient energy to swill it when you got back,' remarked Mr. Drizzle, glancing at the powdery cleanliness of the wheels.

Phillip looked at him. 'Yes, I did. I hadn't cleaned it for week and thought it could do with a swill. It didn't take many minutes.'

'I see. Of course, that would be after you dropped in at the Barrel, wouldn't it?'

'The Barrel?' Phillip regarded Mr. Drizzle curiously. 'What do you mean?'

'You won't remember me,' went on the inspector, unheeding the other's question, 'but I happened to see you go out just after I'd come in. Of course you'd have the car then?'

'Yes, I had.'

'Funny I didn't see it.'

'Nothing funny about that,' said Phillip curtly. 'I left it round the corner.'

'I see.' Mr. Drizzle nodded complacently and Sergeant Ansell took up the interrogation.

'And where had you been before you arrived at the Barrel, then?'

Phillip swung round on him, his temper growing more uncertain every minute. 'Look here,' he said hotly, 'what's all this about? What the deuce have my movements last evening got to do with this burglary? I don't see that it matters a damn where I was last night.'

'Come, come, Mr. Manton,' said Mr. Drizzle softly. 'There's no need to be offended. Suppose we have a look at your study again?'

Phillip complied with alacrity, and they went back to the cottage. They found Mrs. Gribbs in the hall, her narrow face blanched and an expression of abject terror on her features.

'I knew it,' she cried, screwing the corner of her apron viciously between her fingers. 'I knew it. If somethin' dreadful don't 'appen to us all, it'll be a miracle, that's what it'll be!'

Phillip stared at her in amazement. 'Whatever's wrong, Mrs. Gribbs?' he asked, forgetting his anger. 'You look as though you've seen a ghost.'

'I've seen Joe Rodgers, the milkman,' she said, and Mr. Drizzle seemed to have heard that name before. 'It was 'im what did it.'

'But — '

'It was what 'e said,' she went on, continuing her attack on the apron. 'What with burglaries an' murders, it's a wonder we don't all die in our beds. Pore Miss Margery. I allus said somethin' would 'appen at that house.'

Phillip started. 'Margery? Do you mean Miss Trevelyn?' There was a perceptible concern in his voice and Mrs. Gribbs nodded. 'What's happened? She isn't — '

'Oh, no, it isn't 'er. It's 'er uncle. 'E's bin murdered. Found 'im 'anging in the garden, they did.'

'Oh!' Phillip looked relieved. 'But that's nonsense — '

'Is it?' said Mr. Drizzle suddenly. 'Why is it nonsense, Mr. Manton?'

'Eh? Well, I mean — '

'Perhaps Mr. Manton knew he wasn't found hanging,' suggested Ansell sharply. Mrs. Gribbs ceased her wringing operations on the apron and regarded them quizzically.

114

'As sure as I'm standin' 'ere, that's what young Joe Rodgers said when 'e brought the milk this mornin',' she declared. 'An' 'e's courtin' one of the 'ousemaids up there, so 'e orter know. 'Angin' by a rope from one of the trees, 'e said.'

'Then Joe seems to have a nasty habit of exaggerating things,' said Mr. Drizzle. 'Mr. Trevelyn was found in his study, strangled by a silk scarf. Those are the actual facts, Mr. Manton.'

'Are you sure — I mean — '

'We don't usually make mistakes in matters of murder, Mr. Manton,' said the stocky man dryly.

'Of course not,' Phillip agreed. 'But it's so horrible. Why, whoever would want to murder a man like Trevelyn?'

Ansell fixed him with a stare. 'That's what we want to find out, Mr. Manton,' he said. 'And that's also why we were anxious about your movements last night. You see, we know all about your recent quarrel with Mr. Trevelyn, and up to now, you seem to be the only person who has sufficient reason for wanting him out of the way.'

Phillip stared at him in amazement. 'Are you mad?' he asked. 'Why,' he laughed, 'the idea's preposterous. Because I happen to have a ridiculous quarrel with Mr. Trevelyn, is that to say I should want to murder him?'

'That depends,' said Ansell coolly, 'on whether you had sufficient courage to carry out the threats you made.'

Phillip reddened. 'So you've heard about that, have you? You must have been into this affair pretty deeply. Yes, I did threaten Mr. Trevelyn — but what I said or how much I said, I can't tell you. If you've ever lost your temper, you'll realize how much you can say that you're sorry for afterwards.'

Mrs. Gribbs, who had been watching them with wide, staring eyes, nodded; and Phillip, to get out of earshot of that inquisitive individual, walked into the study. They followed him inside and Phillip shut the door, much to the annoyance and disappointment of Mrs. Gribbs.

'So I'm chief suspect, am I?' he said lightly. He smiled. 'It may interest you to know that for the greater part of last evening, I was with Miss Trevelyn — in this study.'

'What were you doing?'

'Most of the time, carrying on an ordinary conversation. And the rest, I was trying to write.'

'With Miss Trevelyn here?' Ansell's tone was sarcastic.

'Yes. She was helping me; she often does. I'm working on a new novel at present, and as the plot was partly her idea, she was reading some of it over.'

Phillip stopped and stared hard at Mr. Drizzle, who was leaning by the side of the desk. While they had been talking, the Scotland Yard man had picked up a thick wad of typescript, and he was flicking through the pages interestedly.

'Is this your new novel, Mr. Manton?' he asked.

'Yes.' Phillip hastily crossed the room and held out his hand. 'I'd better put that away — '

'Just a minute,' said the stocky man slowly. 'I think this is rather peculiar.' He passed the sheets over to Ansell. 'Have a look at those.'

The stout sergeant took them and glanced at the top page impatiently. 'Why bother about a manuscript?' he exclaimed irritably. 'I didn't think you — '

He broke off with a gasp as he read the typewritten characters. 'Good Lord! Why — '

Phillip snatched the papers out of his hands. 'I don't know what this is all about,' he said hotly, 'but I like your infernal cheek! Perhaps you'll be good enough to explain yourselves?'

'Certainly I'll explain,' said Mr. Drizzle softly. 'But I rather think you'll have to do a little of that. I don't suppose you intended us to see that manuscript, did you? *The Silk Scarf Crime*. Quite a topical title, isn't it? Especially when the story concerns a character who's murdered by a silk scarf. Might have been taken from real life. Or was it the other way about, Mr. Manton? Was the real life taken from fiction?'

All the colour drained from Phillip Manton' face, and he swayed slightly on his feet. His experience of last night, coupled with the startling development, was beginning to take its toll, and he felt faint.

'If you're insinuating that I'm responsible for the ghastly affair,' he gasped, 'you're mistaken.'

'Then perhaps you can explain why Mr. Trevelyn came to be murdered in exactly the same way as the character in your story, Mr. Manton,' said the Scotland Yard man.

'I can't. It must be a coincidence — '

'Coincidences like that don't happen.'

'Then I can't tell you. All I can say is that I didn't do it.'

'Perhaps you can tell us who did?' suggest Ansell, and Phillip stared. 'You said that part of this plot was Miss Trevelyn's idea. Perhaps — '

'Are you really crazy?' flashed Phillip angrily. 'Do you think she'd murder her own uncle?'

'He was killed by her scarf.'

'And of course, that makes her the murderer!' snorted the young man sarcastically. 'Brilliant deduction by local police sergeant! Good heavens!'

Ansell flushed deeply and his anger

rose. 'Instead of being insulting, Mr. Manton,' he said, 'I suggest you get ready to accompany us to the police station. We may have to detain you pending inquiries.'

The shock of this statement calmed Phillip considerably, and he stared at the sergeant coolly. 'You can't arrest me. You've absolutely no proof that I killed Matthew Trevelyn. The fact that the plot of my story coincides exactly with the way in which he was murdered isn't proof that I'm responsible — or Margery either.'

Ansell bit his lip, and his colour deepened.

'You are here to investigate a burglary,' went on Phillip, icily, 'and I should be extremely pleased if you would get on with the business. Regarding the murder, I know nothing about it, and, until you can furnish me with conclusive proof that I do, I wish to say nothing about the matter.'

Ansell snorted angrily and shot a glance at Mr. Drizzle. The stocky man shook his head, and the sergeant, realizing that he could do nothing but capitulate, dropped the manuscript on the desk.

10

The Double Heart

After a tiring morning, there's nothing more refreshing than a cool glass of well-conditioned beer; and Sergeant Ansell, who did not deny that it had been a tiring morning, accepted Mr. Drizzle's invitation with alacrity.

Investigation into the burglary had been fruitless, and as there was nothing to be found that constituted anything in the way of a clue, they left Briar Cottage little wiser than when they had come. But it wasn't that that was worrying Ansell. From the incidents that morning, he had become quite convinced that Phillip Manton knew far more about the murder than he pretended — but he realized that until they could produce further proof to that effect, they were powerless. They could, of course, have arrested Manton on suspicion; but Mr. Drizzle, to whose intervention the young author owed his present liberty, knew quite well that had they done so, they would have had to release him again within a couple of hours. Consequently, Sergeant Ansell was not in the best of tempers.

Arriving in the small high street, the car stopped beneath the gently swaying sign of the Barrel Inn; and Sergeant Ansell, with one grateful look at the half-timbered building, got out and followed Mr. Drizzle into the cool bar-parlour. The place was empty; and Mr. Balmer, who by rights should have been washing up the few glasses that had been used that morning, was sprawled over one end of the counter, perusing with apparent eagerness his latest acquisition from Mr. Gregg.

Mr. Balmer looked up. 'Wotcher want?' he demanded.

Mr. Drizzle said they would like two beers if he didn't mind; and the landlord, who looked as though he did, reluctantly laid down his book and rose to get them. Mr. Drizzle glanced at the illustrated dust jacket.

'One of Mr. Manton's books. I see,' he remarked, and the landlord nodded.

'Latest,' he replied shortly. 'Rare good 'un it is, too. Fair makes your flesh creep. Almost as if Mr. Manton 'ad experienced it 'imself.' He came back with the beers and pushed them over the counter. 'But I thought you were the gent last night what said 'e didn't like thrillers?'

Mr. Drizzle nodded. 'I am.'

'Gentleman who asked for Friar's Lodge?'

Mr. Drizzle nodded again, and the landlord regarded him with renewed interest. 'Then you'll be that detective chap from Scotland Yard who's mixed up with this business at Friar's Lodge?' he ventured.

With a smile, Mr. Drizzle admitted that distinction, at the same time wondering how on earth he had got hold of that — and the landlord shook his head.

'Awful business, that,' he commented, picking up his book and flicking abstractedly through its pages. 'Just like somethin' out of one of Mr. Manton's stories.'

The stocky man agreed that it was, and took a long drink from his glass. Half empty, he placed it on the counter again, and congratulated Mr. Balmer on the excellence of his beer. Mr. Balmer was gratified, and became effusive in his gratitude, and before long had been drawn into an interesting conversation concerning Phillip Manton. It was only then that Ansell realized the reason for Mr. Drizzle's sudden thirst, and the sergeant left him to it.

It could not be denied that Mr. Balmer was talkative; his loquacity was, in fact, astounding, and Mr. Drizzle, who knew how to handle such individuals, found Mr. Balmer a very interesting person. Much of what he said was pure gossip, composed of little fact and much imagination, and could safely be taken with the proverbial grain of salt. But one fact was evident. Phillip Manton was popular. Mr. Balmer had not a single word to say against him, and his demeanour suggested that anyone who had would have him to reckon with. Whereupon Ansell, with his glass to his lips, expressed his feelings in a grunt. Ansell did not agree.

'Where did he come from, then?' asked

Mr. Drizzle casually, producing his pipe and charging it with that villainous-looking mixture of his. 'Hasn't been here long, has he?'

Mr. Balmer shook his head. 'Nigh on fourteen months, I believe. But I can't tell you where 'e come from. Sort of just appeared, 'e did. 'E'd been livin' in Briar Cottage a week before anyone knew 'e was there. 'Ad the 'ouse done up in no time, too, then built a garage for that car of 'is.' Mr. Balmer shook his head regretfully. 'Pity 'e ever got that car. Somethin' 'ull 'appen to it as sure as eggs. Course, it's all the same with these young chaps, but a bit more with Mr. Manton, I say. Not that 'e ain't a good driver — 'e is; but 'e's got what 'e calls a taste for speed, an' with roads like them what we 'ave round 'ere, one don't want no speed. Nearly 'ad a do last night, 'e 'ad.'

'Oh?' Mr. Drizzle paused in the act of striking a match and glanced at the landlord interestedly. 'When was that?'

'Just afore you came, sir. Mr. Manton came in lookin' somethin' awful. 'Is face was as white as a sheet an' 'e was

125

tremblin' like a leaf. 'Ad a nasty skid in 'is car, 'e said, and run into a ditch. Asked for a double whisky, 'e did, and believe me, 'e could do with it.'

Mr. Drizzle lit his pipe and pulled at it in silence for a few moments. So Mr. Manton had had a skid in his car, had he? Come into the pub looking very shaken and asked for a double whisky? Somehow that didn't sound right to Mr. Drizzle. Looking at the car, as he had done that morning, there had been no signs of a skid or anything else. And that double whisky . . . A stimulant of that nature was usually taken to restore one's jagged nerves, and after committing a murder . . . The idea occurred simultaneously to Sergeant Ansell, and a glance was exchanged between them.

At that moment, another customer entered the bar; and Mr. Drizzle, taking the opportunity to conclude the conversation, paid for the drinks, and with Ansell passed into the street.

'Well?' It was Ansell who spoke, but there was little interrogation in his tone. 'What do you think now?'

Mr. Drizzle did not reply until they were seated in the car. 'I think it's about time we got back to the police station,' he said. 'I'm feeling ready for lunch.'

Ansell clicked his teeth in annoyance. 'About Phillip Manton, I mean. Surely you don't believe that rot about the car, do you?'

'I don't believe anything I'm told,' Mr. Drizzle said sententiously, 'especially when it comes from such individuals as mine host! All the same, I admit it looks fishy.'

'Fishy isn't the word,' grunted Ansell, settling his extensive figure comfortably in the upholstered seat. 'Something happened to upset Manton last night, and I'm damned sure it wasn't the car. I looked at it pretty carefully this morning, and apart from seeing that he had recently given it a thorough swill down, there wasn't the least sign of a skid.'

Mr. Drizzle nodded. It certainly looked peculiar. As a motorist himself, he knew quite well how impossible it was to go through a skid, no matter how small, without leaving traces, if only to the tyres; and the tyres had been as good as new. No,

Phillip Manton had lied — that was evident — and as far as he could see, to only one purpose. Yet . . . somewhere inside him, Mr. Drizzle had a curious feeling that it was all wrong. Despite the growing evidence against young Manton, the detective found it hard to believe he was a murderer. His looks, his personality, everything about him were in complete contrast to such an idea, and a vague doubt began to manifest itself upon his wavering conviction. And the burglary . . . Mr. Drizzle shot a quick glance at Ansell.

'If he *was* responsible for the murder, then what about the burglary?' he asked suddenly as the idea struck him.

'Burglary? What do you mean?'

'How do you account for it?'

'I don't,' replied Ansell with emphatic promptness. 'I don't believe there was one.'

Mr. Drizzle looked at him in surprise. 'What on earth do you mean? Why, that's rot!'

'Is it?' said Ansell. 'Listen — there was no trace of anyone having entered, was there? There was nothing missing. In fact, there was nothing to show that there had been a burglary at all.'

'Only the bandage round Manton's head,' Mr. Drizzle reminded him as he set the car moving down the street.

'How do we know what was beneath that bandage?'

'Well, Mrs. Gribbs saw — '

'With a little imagination, a drop of red ink, and a bit of play-acting, it shouldn't be very difficult to delude a woman like Mrs. Gribbs.'

Mr. Drizzle pondered. 'All right, then,' he conceded. 'Suppose the burglary was faked. To what purpose was it done?'

For a few seconds, Sergeant Ansell maintained a cogitative silence, then: 'There's only one reason I can think of. It was done to throw us off the scent.'

'Off the scent?' Mr. Drizzle's tone was incredulous above the gentle hum of the car. 'How?'

'Well . . . ' Ansell floundered. Obviously his theory had not met with the success he had hoped. 'He must have known we should suspect him.'

'Of course.'

'And he must have known we should go to see him.'

'Well?'

'Well, then, he faked this burglary, hoping we should think it had been committed by the same person who killed Matthew Trevelyn, and therefore put him out of the running.'

The theory was the flimsiest Mr. Drizzle had ever heard, and the expression with which he received it intimated as much. Had they not at that moment pulled up before the police station, the Scotland Yard man would have taken infinite pleasure in pulling it to pieces. Instead, he gave a noncommittal grunt and alighted from the car.

Inside the police station, they found that Colonel Wade had gone, much to the unconcealed satisfaction of Sergeant Ansell, but another visitor in the person of Dr. Westwood was waiting to see them instead.

''Morning, Ansell,' he greeted as they entered the sergeant's cramped office. 'I've got that report here.' He tapped some papers on the desk. 'Hardly more than what I told you last night. This is an official version, that's all.'

Ansell nodded and picked up the sheets. 'There'll be an inquest, of course?'

'Of course. I've arranged that for tomorrow.'

The doctor looked at Mr. Drizzle. 'You'll be staying for that, won't you?'

Mr. Drizzle nodded. 'I shall — and after that, too. I'm giving the sergeant my — er — my assistance with the case.'

'M'm!' Westwood raised his eyes doubtfully. 'Well, I wish you luck.' He leaned on Ansell's desk. 'It's a funny thing — I've been Trevelyn's doctor for years, and I never knew he had a birthmark.'

'A what?' said Ansell, looking up.

'Yes.' The doctor smiled. 'It's a funny little thing. Shaped like a double heart, and under the left arm, too.'

Mr. Drizzle started. 'Say that again, will you?'

'What? About the birthmark?' The doctor complied. 'A little red mark the shape of a double heart under the left arm.'

The stocky man nodded. 'I get you,' he

said. 'A double heart. A double heart. Now where have I heard that before?' He pulled absently at his lower lip as he strove to capture the vague thread of memory that had suddenly been loosened. 'It's funny. I've heard that before somewhere.' He came to a sudden decision. 'Can I use your telephone?'

'Eh? Of course,' said Ansell. 'But what — '

Mr. Drizzle grabbed at the receiver. 'I'm getting through to Scotland Yard,' he explained. 'Somewhere, sometime, in circumstances I can't remember, I've come up against that double heart. And if they haven't got something about it in Records, then I'm a Dutchman!'

11

Something in the Past

Mr. Drizzle had spent quite a busy afternoon. Sometime after lunch, a very disreputable figure in a pair of exceedingly dirty overalls had arrived at Friar's Lodge and announced to the somewhat disapproving Grasset, who had answered his strident peal on the doorbell, that he was from the local G.P.O. After a brief inspection of the telephone, wire he had finally succeeded in discovering the defect. The break had occurred in a part of the wire which ran through a cupboard under the stairs, and quite a considerable portion of it had been removed. In itself, this information wasn't much, but it contributed substantially towards Ansell's evidence against Phillip Manton. For it could mean only one thing: whoever had cut that wire must have had some knowledge of the inside of the house, as the cupboard, in the true manner of all understairs cupboards, was unobtrusive; and unless one had definitely known about it, its presence would never have been suspected. And young Manton, reminded Sergeant Ansell, had been quite a frequent visitor.

There had been very little other information. The doctor's report, a purely technical statement, meant nothing. Trevelyn had been strangled and that was all there was to it. What few fingerprints they had taken were also useless, for on examination, they found that they belonged only to Trevelyn himself and the rest of the household. And an inspection of the grounds had met with similar results, for of the man on the terrace there was not the slightest trace.

All of which was very unsatisfactory. Alhough they had searched Matthew Trevelyn's study from top to bottom, gone through every drawer and cupboard, and looked at every scrap of paper there was to look at, they had found nothing.

Mr. Drizzle, who was sitting smoking with his chair by the open window of the drawing room, was pondering over this peculiar point when he heard someone enter. He looked round and saw that it was Margery.

'Hello!' she said. 'Where — where's the sergeant?'

'Ansell?' Mr. Drizzle moved his chair back a little. 'He's gone. He'll be back later, though. I'm afraid he's rather disappointed. We've been through all your uncle's effects, but we haven't found a thing. We'll have to rely on you to tell us what you can about him, that's all.'

'About him?' She looked at the detective in surprise. 'How do you mean?'

'About his past life, I mean. That's very important, you know.'

She creased her forehead into an attractive little wrinkle. 'Then I'm afraid I'll be no more use to you than your search has been. I know very little about him.'

Mr. Drizzle stared. 'Your uncle?' He was surprised. 'But surely . . . Your family life . . . '

'There hasn't been any,' she replied. 'Uncle Matthew has always been rather cut off from our family life — at least,' she added, 'as far as I was concerned. Until four years ago, I'd never even met him.'

'Oh?' Mr. Drizzle permitted himself to raise his eyebrows slightly. 'Perhaps if you'd tell me . . . '

Margery strolled slowly across to the window and gazed outside. As the light fell squarely on her small oval face, Mr. Drizzle noticed that her expression was grimly thoughtful, and he sensed a story worth listening to.

'I'm afraid my uncle had been something of a mystery to me,' she said as she curled snugly in a corner of the window seat. 'Daddy hardly ever used to mention him, but from what he did occasionally say, I gathered that he had been rather a bad hat. That surprises you, doesn't it?' She turned her head as she caught a glimpse of wonderment on Mr. Drizzle's usually impassive countenance. 'It did me when I met him. All my life I'd been led to believe that he was something of a rotter, but when I came to live with him I found that there wasn't a dearer old man breathing. He wasn't *really* old, you know. Not quite fifty, I believe, but he looked a great deal older than he was. Anyway, I liked him tremendously, and I just can't believe he was as bad as Daddy used to think.'

Mr. Drizzle nodded. 'And why was your uncle supposed to be such a bad hat? I mean, what had he done?'

She shook her head. 'I don't know. I was never told. But whatever it was it happened a very long time ago; before I was born, anyhow. The family lost sight of him for quite a while, I believe.'

'I see,' said Mr. Drizzle. 'Then you know very little about him at all?'

'I know nothing, actually.'

'H'm! Then how did you come to live with him? I mean, if he was such a rogue and you had never seen him before?'

She smiled. 'I thought you'd ask that. It's very simple, really. You see, Uncle Matthew was the only living relative I had left — Mother died when I was quite young — and when Daddy died suddenly four years ago, I was left without a friend in the world. Of course I was at school then, but six months later I finished my education, and I was in the unhappy position of not having a home to go to. I had some money — Daddy left everything to me — and there was the house, but of course that was no good to me. I couldn't live by myself. Then Uncle Matthew stepped in, and as Daddy's brother, he became a sort of guardian. He had just bought this house, he said, and he insisted that I should come to live with him, and — well, I had no option. I was very frightened at first, as I'd never seen him before; and the impression I had gathered concerning him didn't help to make things easier, either. But I think he understood that, for he was very kind to me and I was really grateful for what he did.'

'M'm!' Mr. Drizzle ran the stem of his pipe across his lower lip. 'That's very interesting. I wish we could find out something more about him. There seems to be a strange absence of papers among his belongings.' He looked up suddenly. 'Did he ever receive any correspondence?'

She shook her head. 'Not often. He did sometimes, of course. But that was only when the vicar was away or something like that.'

'I see. And did he have any lately, do you know?'

'Well . . . ' She pondered. 'As a matter of fact, he did. He had quite a few this last week or so.'

'Oh?' Mr. Drizzle looked at her sharply. 'That's interesting — very interesting. Do you know what they were about?'

'I don't.'

'Or where they came from?'

'I'm sorry.'

'M'm! That's a pity. You don't know what became of them, I suppose?'

She frowned as she rose to her feet. 'I don't know really, of course, but — but I've an idea he burned them.'

'Burned them?'

'Yes.'

'What makes you think that?'

'Well, I began to notice that soon after he received a letter, there was generally some charred paper in the fire-grate in his study. It may not have been the letters he burned, but certainly he burned something.' She sighed as she began to move across the room. 'I'm sorry I haven't been very helpful. You'll let me know if there's anything else I can do, won't you?'

Mr. Drizzle nodded, and his brow contracted in a deep frown.

'I'll let you know,' he said.

12

An Unpleasant Shock

Phillip Manton pulled the sheet from the typewriter, read a few of the atrociously typed lines, then screwed it into a ball and flung it disgustedly into the wastepaper basket.

'Hang!' he muttered savagely. He rammed the carriage of his machine back to the centre and rose to mix himself a whisky-and-soda.

He poured out the drink with a hand that was none too steady, splashed in a minimum of soda, then walked over to the window and gazed out. A cool breeze, fragrant with the faint scent of roses, stirred the stuffy air of the room, and he was grateful. His head ached damnably and maybe it would help to ease it a little. Instinctively his hand fingered the bandage over his throbbing head, and he cursed the unknown visitor of the night before.

Swallowing most of the drink at a gulp, he turned back to his desk and sat down again. It was no good trying to concentrate on writing, he told himself, glancing ruefully at the well-filled wastepaper basket. His mind was in too much of a whirl to contend with fiction, and he found it hard enough to comprehend fact at the moment. Stretching out his hand, he explored the confines of his littered desk and presently found his cigarettes. Lighting one, he leaned back in his chair and inhaled the cool smoke gratefully.

Heavens, he *was* in a mess. If it hadn't been for that damned manuscript, he might have bluffed things out. But now, however, they were bound to suspect him. Of course, they would make investigations, and when they did . . .

He started suddenly as the familiar squeak of his front gate cut into his thoughts. Confound it, they weren't coming already . . . ? Rising impatiently from his seat, he crossed to the window. If they were . . . His expression changed suddenly as he saw the slim form of Margery Trevelyn hurrying up the path, and, tossing his cigarette into the hearth, he dashed into the hall to meet her.

'Margery,' he cried, holding out his arms as she stepped through the open front door. 'I'm so glad you're here. I thought I should *never* see you.'

'Oh, Phillip . . . ' He felt her small body tremble as he took her in his arms. 'Phillip, I had to come. You — you know — ?'

'Yes.' He nodded. 'I know. In fact, I should think the whole village knows by now. There's no need to say how sorry I am; you know that. But do come inside. You look absolutely worn out.'

He released his hold upon her and led her into the study. 'If there's anything you'd like — '

'No, thank you. I'm quite all right.' She supported herself wearily against the desk, and Phillip moved to get her a chair. 'But — but you — ' She looked in alarm at the bandage around his head. 'You're hurt. Oh, Phillip, they told me, but I didn't think — '

'Oh, this?' Phillip fingered his head. 'It's nothing, really. I'm all right — '

'You — you're sure — ?'

'Absolutely. It's only a scratch. Apart from a beastly headache, I'm perfectly all right. It's you I've been worrying about. You're sure there's nothing I can get you? A cocktail? Or perhaps you'd like some tea?'

'No. There's nothing, thank you.' She shook her head, and once again Phillip noticed how terribly pale and tired she looked. 'As a matter of fact . . . ' She hesitated.

'Yes?' he prompted gently.

'Well, I really came here this afternoon to — to ask you something. Something that intimately concerns us both, Phillip. Oh, I've — I've worried all day until I could see you and find out the truth.' She bit her lip, and her knuckles showed white as she gripped the back of the chair in an effort to control her feelings. Then: 'You remember a few days ago when you asked me to — to — '

He nodded. He didn't suppose he'd ever forget that day.

'I left my scarf on the desk — the green silk one, you know. You wanted to turn

144

back for it but I wanted to tell Uncle as soon as we could. You remember?'

'Why, yes,' he said in surprise. 'But what — '

'May I — may I have it back, please?' There was something like desperation in her tone. 'It's — it's terribly important, really, or I wouldn't have asked you. *Please.*'

Phillip looked at her in astonishment. Whatever did she mean? He was utterly at a loss to analyse her motive for such a request, but so urgent was her tone that he hesitated only a second, then went over to the desk and opened one of the drawers.

'Mrs. Gribbs probably found it yesterday,' he remarked as he rummaged about. 'She'll have put it in here, I suppose. At least . . . '

'Then I'm afraid you won't find it there now,' said Margery quietly.

Phillip raised his head and looked at her in puzzlement. 'Why not?' he asked. 'But you're right, you know. It certainly isn't here. Yet Mrs. Gribbs generally shoves everything in this drawer when she's cleaning up.'

'You needn't bother to look any further, Phillip,' she said, and her voice trembled. 'I can tell you where it is. It — it's at home, at Friar's Lodge.'

'Friar's Lodge?' echoed Phillip. 'But how on earth'

He didn't finish the sentence. Suddenly, awfully, he heard the smooth tones of that stocky policeman saying: *'Mr Trevelyn was found in his study — strangled by a silk scarf. Those are the facts, Mr. Manton . . . '*

'Good God!' he breathed. 'Your uncle — '

The next second, Margery was in his arms sobbing softly.

'It doesn't matter what the whole world thinks so long as you believe me,' he told her. He gazed unseeingly over her tousled hair and his lips drew together in a tight, hard line. 'Margery, I give you my word that I haven't seen that scarf since the day you brought it. I imagined Mrs. Gribbs would put it in the top drawer when she cleaned up — she usually does. Anyway, I'd forgotten all about it. How it got where — where you say it is now, I don't know. You trust me, don't you?'

'Of course I do. You know that,' she said. 'But Sergeant Ansell knows I left my scarf here. Phillip, I'm dreadfully frightened as to what he might think. He — he may — '

Phillip whistled inaudibly. 'Ansell knows, does he? Lord, that's awkward. On top of what happened this morning, he may do anything — '

'Happened this morning?' She looked at him anxiously. 'Of course they came to see you, didn't they?'

'They did. And that's what I mean. They know about the story. The one we planned out together. They were in here this morning, and that other little chap happened to pick up the manuscript. It never occurred to me or I should never have been fool enough to leave it lying about, but your uncle . . . it was done in exactly the same way as the story. You remember *The Silk Scarf Crime* we called it, and we got the idea from your scarf. What damning evidence!' He moved restlessly about the room.

'Then thank goodness,' breathed Margery, 'that I told them I'd collected it again.'

Phillip stopped. 'You told them that?' He looked at her strangely. 'You told them that it wasn't left here after all?'

Margery nodded. 'What else could I do? I — I was terrified. Things looked so — so awful against you. So I had to tell them something — though I don't know whether they believed me. Oh, Phillip, what if they should find out? What if they should arrest you?'

'I don't think they would — at least, not on that. But Lord knows, with that and the manuscript, there's enough evidence to put a mighty black case against me in a court of justice. But they can't really arrest me until they can prove that I *was* at Friar's Lodge — no matter what they suspect.'

'Of course.' Margery's face brightened somewhat. 'Then — then there's nothing really to worry about. If you weren't at Friar's Lodge last night, they can't possibly prove that you were, can they?'

He didn't answer for a moment but stared broodingly at the mass of papers in his desk. Margery went to his side.

'They can't — can they?' she said

slowly. He turned to her and placed a gentle hand on her arm.

'I'm afraid they might,' he said heavily, and he frowned. 'Terribly afraid. I'm sorry if this is going to shock you, Margery, but you see, I — I was there . . . '

Margery gasped. Her face paled and she looked at him in horror. 'You were there?'

'Yes. I went straight after you left here — ' He broke off suddenly as he heard a movement behind them.

'That's very interesting, Mr. Manton,' said a voice — a cool, almost sleepy voice that he remembered quite well. 'Very interesting indeed. I'd like to hear more about that. Do you mind if I come in?'

They both swung round in amazement, and Mr. Drizzle, who had been leaning through the open window, walked to the front door.

13

Mr. Drizzle Collects Some Facts

For some dreadful seconds, Phillip Manton stared at the open window as though he had seen a ghost. Visions of blue-coated policemen, jingling handcuffs and solemn-toned warnings flashed through his stunned mind, and he was barely conscious that Margery was clinging to him in terror. He stared dumbly at Mr. Drizzle as the stocky man entered the study and nodded pleasantly. Then at last, after what seemed an eternity, the young writer found his voice.

'What the — what the devil are you doing here?' he demanded brusquely, and his tone sounded hoarse and unnatural to his ears.

'I came to see you,' replied Mr. Drizzle smoothly. He seemed quite oblivious of the sensation he had caused. 'I'd no idea you had a visitor. I knocked twice, but you apparently didn't hear, so, as the house seemed sort of open, I thought I'd better — er — investigate, as it were. I don't eavesdrop as a rule, you know, but I must say you've saved me quite a lot of trouble.'

'Lot of trouble — ?'

'Yes. It was going to be rather awkward to prove that you were at Friar's Lodge last night — though it was pretty evident, wasn't it?'

'Look here,' cried Phillip suddenly. 'Who the deuce are you?'

Mr. Drizzle raised his eyebrows. 'Hasn't Miss Trevelyn told you?' he asked. 'Pity, because I hate introductions. However, here's my card.'

Margery relinquished her hold on Phillip's arm and he accepted the card mechanically. 'Scotland Yard?' he said slowly. 'But I still don't understand — '

'Inspector Drizzle came down to Friar's Lodge last night,' put in Margery. 'Uncle Matthew had sent for him. He arrived just after I had — had found him.'

Mr. Drizzle nodded gratefully. 'So you see,' he said with a smile, 'that explains everything, doesn't it? I've no doubt you thought me quite an interfering old buffer this morning.'

Phillip breathed hard and looked at the other steadily. 'All right,' he said resignedly. 'How much have you heard?'

'Very little really,' confessed the stocky man regretfully. 'You were just telling Miss Trevelyn that you were at Friar's Lodge last night. That's rather a dangerous statement, you know.'

'You'll have a job to prove — '

'Oh, come, Mr. Manton,' said Mr. Drizzle wearily. 'Don't you think you're behaving very unwisely? Why don't you tell me what you know?'

'And help you to put a rope round my neck?' said Phillip testily.

Mr. Drizzle looked at him. 'What makes you think I'm trying to put a rope round your neck?' he asked.

'Well — '

'On the contrary, I'm doing my best to loosen it. You're in a tough position, Mr. Manton, and I need hardly disguise the fact, but I should hate to see you make a mess of things by being obstinate. I'll be frank with you. I don't believe you did kill

Matthew Trevelyn.'

Margery stared. Phillip looked at him amazement. Coming from a policeman, this was the strangest thing he'd ever heard.

'You don't — *what*?'

'I'm a great believer in common intelligence,' went on Mr. Drizzle, 'and unless I'm very mistaken you have quite a lot of that. Therefore, I hardly think you'd be crass enough to commit a murder in exactly the same way as one of your stories — not if you value that neck of yours, anyway. So what about it?'

Phillip studied him for a moment. Somehow, despite the peculiarity of the situation, he felt himself liking this little man. He was so utterly different from the policemen he used in his books. He came to a sudden decision.

'All right,' he said. 'I'll lay my cards on the table. Yes, I was at Friar's Lodge last night.'

Margery clutched at his arm, and Mr. Drizzle nodded.

'Carry on, Mr. Manton. I know that bit. Why did you go?'

'I wanted to see Margery's uncle.'

'Did Miss Trevelyn know?'

Phillip shook his head. 'No. I didn't decide until after she'd gone.'

'Oh? And what made you decide then?'

'Oh, I don't know.' Phillip mechanically reached for his open packet of cigarettes and began to tap one of them on his thumbnail. 'An impulse, I suppose you'd call it.'

'I see. And what was the cause of this — er — impulse?'

Phillip seated himself on the edge of the desk before replying. Then: 'You've heard about our quarrel, I suppose?' Mr. Drizzle nodded. 'Well, I wanted to see him about that. He said some pretty rotten things that night — things that I couldn't understand; and I suddenly made up my mind to get to the bottom of it. Of course, he'd forbidden me to go anywhere near the house, I know, but in the heat of the moment — '

The inspector nodded again. 'I understand that, Mr. Manton. But surely you knew that Mr. Trevelyn had been confined to bed all day?'

'Oh yes,' said Phillip. He struck a match and lighted his cigarette. 'I knew that. Margery told me. But I thought that by that time he might have got up again.'

Mr. Drizzle raised his eyebrows. He glance across at Margery, and she nodded. 'That's perfectly correct,' she agreed. 'Uncle was like that. He was very susceptible to colds, as I told you last night I believe, and at the first sign of one he'd stay in bed. Generally he'd get up for an hour or two in the evening if he felt all right.'

Mr. Drizzle signified his understanding with a nod, then went back to Phillip. 'So you got your car out, eh?' he suggested.

'That's right,' said Phillip. 'I thought it would be quicker that way, and I did want to see him before Margery got back. I had some wild idea of being able to straighten things out, I remember, but — ' He laughed, but there was little mirth in his tone. ' — as things turned out, I was too late. Anyway, it didn't take me long; I was there within five minutes.'

'I see. And what happened then?'

'I left my car at the gates and walked up the drive. It was very dark, and

— well, I didn't know why, but the place seemed deserted, I thought. I mean, there weren't any lights about — not at the front, at least. However, I rang the bell and waited. There was no reply, so I rang again. I almost began to wish that I hadn't come, for I had no idea what I was going to say to Margery's uncle when I saw him. I rang three or four times, I believe, but there was still no answer, so I was forced to the conclusion that Mr. Trevelyn had not got up after all. I mean, if he had he would most certainly have answered the door if the servants had been unable to. And what had become of the servants I couldn't imagine, but it was pretty evident that they were nowhere about.

'However, having by this time just about rung the house down as well as banging the door in, I decided that there was nothing more to do but to go home, so I set off down the drive again.' He paused and flicked the end of his cigarette into the well-used ashtray. 'It was only when I was about halfway down the drive that I happened to turn round and see the light. Whether it had been on when I had gone up the drive I don't know, but certainly it was on then, and as it came from the side of the house I knew it was in Mr. Trevelyn's study. Of course, I went back. It was beastly dark and it took me some time to get round, but finally I reached the terrace. I saw that the French windows were open and the light was full on, and — and — ' Phillip paused.

'Well?'

'I was just about to go in when *someone came out.*'

Margery gasped. 'Someone came out?' she echoed. 'Who?'

'I don't know. I couldn't see. But I think they must have heard me coming. Anyway, they dashed out like the very devil and nearly knocked me spinning. Where they went to, I don't know.'

'I see.' Mr. Drizzle regarded him thoughtfully. 'And you say you don't know who he was?'

'I don't,' said Phillip. He expelled a thin stream of tobacco smoke into the room. 'It was pitch dark outside, and the light from the room was very brilliant. I was dazzled for a minute. All I know is that someone brushed past me; but who it was, or where they went, I can't tell you.'

'Very well. And what did you do then?'

'Nothing for a few seconds. I was too surprised. But when I did recover myself, I went into the study. I'd just passed through the windows when — when I saw him . . . '

He paused and looked apologetically at Margery, but her countenance was expressionless.

'He was lying by the corner of the desk, and I knew he was dead. In a job like mine, it's my business to know things like that — and I knew then. His eyes told me.'

'I see. And then what?'

'I bolted,' said Phillip. 'It may sound a pretty rotten thing to have done, I know, but I'm not ashamed. I think nine people out often would have done what I did. I realized at once that there was a dead man before me — a man who had obviously been murdered — and I appeared to be the only one on the spot. If I'd been caught, I should have been suspected immediately — and that was enough for me. I bolted across that garden like a frightened kid and made straight for my car. I was pretty scared, I can tell you, so I stopped at the Barrel Inn for a bracer. I was in such a rotten state that I had to pitch some tale to old Balmer about the car. I told him I'd had a skid, or — or something. Anyway, it satisfied him. After that, I went straight home, and here I've been ever since. That's all I can tell you.'

'H'm!' Mr. Drizzle rubbed the side of his nose and nodded. 'There's one more thing you've forgotten, you know. Your car. Why did you swill it?'

Phillip smiled and squashed his cigarette in the ashtray. 'It's a habit I've acquired through writing detective stories, I suppose. I did that as a precaution. You may not have noticed, but for once the county council have been doing something to improve the roads in these parts. To be more explicit, they've been tarring and pebbling quite a stretch of it not far from Friar's Lodge — and I went clean through it. I noticed afterwards when I was putting the car away that the tyres showed considerable traces of it — and I wasn't taking any chances.'

Mr. Drizzle nodded. 'I see. And there's nothing more you can tell me?'

'Nothing.'

14

Mr. Drizzle Has an Idea

'Very well.' The Scotland Yard man turned to Margery. 'And now, about that scarf of yours. When was it you left it here?'

Margery caught her breath and looked at him in alarm. 'What — what do you mean?' she asked. 'I told you'

'You told me quite a lot of things, my dear,' broke in Mr. Drizzle with a smile. 'You know, Miss Trevelyn, nature never meant you for lying. You do it so badly. You did leave it here, didn't you?'

'I thought Margery told you last night that she didn't?' cut in Phillip.

'Exactly,' agreed the inspector. 'That's what she told me. But I know that she did leave her scarf here all the same.'

'How — '

'Mr. Manton,' went on the detective in that slow, compelling tone of his, 'you've

161

told me quite a lot this afternoon. Are you going to hamper things by denying a small fact I know to be true?'

Phillip bit his lip. 'Oh, very well,' he said. 'I might as well give you the whole lot. Yes, Margery did leave it here.'

Mr. Drizzle nodded. 'I know that bit. When was it?'

'The day of the quarrel. Margery and I had just become engaged, and we were anxious to inform her uncle of the fact and obtain his approval. We never thought about the scarf when we left here. We'd got almost to Friar's Lodge before we remembered it.'

'M'm! And what became of it?'

'Oh, I don't know,' said the young author vaguely. 'I've never seen it since. I suppose Mrs. Gribbs would find it.'

'I see.' Mr. Drizzle puckered his eyebrows thoughtfully. 'Did you ask her?' Phillip shook his head.

'Then we'd better do so now. Do you mind calling her?'

Phillip did so, and Mrs. Gribbs entered the room. But she declared emphatically that she ''adn't seen no scarf an' didn't

162

know which one 'e meant. Miss Trevelyn was often leavin' things be'ind.'

Whereupon Mrs. Gribbs departed, and Mr. Drizzle turned to Phillip once more. 'You've no reason to doubt her word, I suppose?'

'Who? Mrs. Gribbs?' Phillip looked surprised. 'Good Lord, no! If she says she hasn't seen it, I suppose she hasn't; though how the deuce it's got where you say it is, I don't know. But — but what are you getting at?' he asked curiously.

The stocky man looked at him carefully. 'I'm getting at this, Mr. Manton. Someone must have known that the scarf was in the house somewhere. Someone, also, must have been here, otherwise they could never have got hold of it. And someone must have taken the scarf on the day Mr. Trevelyn was murdered — yesterday. Now do you see what I mean?'

Phillip nodded. 'Yes, I get you. But I'm afraid it's impossible. I was never out of the house yesterday — except for last night, of course.'

'H'm!' Mr. Drizzle pursed his lips. 'But you had some visitors, hadn't you?'

'Ye-es,' admitted Phillip slowly. 'There was Margery — '

'I mean besides Miss Trevelyn.'

'Oh, yes. I had two or three.'

'Good! You can remember who they were, I suppose?'

'Of course. Let's see.' Phillip began to enumerate them on his fingers. 'There was the Reverend Anthony Ross — he came about the sale of work or garden fete, I believe. Then there was Mrs. Garvice. And old Jimmy Grennock, and — oh yes, there was Mr. Balmer.'

'Mr. Balmer?'

'Yes. That's the lot.'

'I see. Not a very prepossessing crowd, is it? All right. Let's take this Reverend Anthony Somebody first. Who's he?'

'Our local vicar,' said Phillip with a smile. 'But I don't think you need put him on your list of suspects.'

'M'm! Maybe not. What did he want?'

'He came to ask me if I'd give a hand at some church function or other. He didn't stay long.'

'I see. And where did you put him? I mean was he in this room?'

'Oh yes, they all were. I always show visitors in here — when I'm not working, that is.'

'Righto! Who's next? What about Mrs. Garvice? What did she want?'

'She came to see me,' put in Margery. 'She'd been up to the Lodge, but as I wasn't there, she thought she might find me here. She wanted me to call at Mr. Gregg's shop for her tonight, as she was going away.'

'Oh! And was she alone for any length of time?'

Phillip pondered. 'Yes . . . she was. Margery was getting tidied in the bathroom when she called. She must have been in this room about five minutes.'

Mr. Drizzle nodded. 'I see. And what about Mr. Grennock, or whatever you called him?'

'Oh, my publisher? He'd come down from London to see me about my new novel. I'm overdue with it. It should have been in last month, and he told me so in no uncertain manner. He's a good chap, you know, but I'll give you a tip in case you ever take to writing novels. Don't be

165

overdue with your work — where Jimmy Grennock is concerned, at least. He didn't stop long, either. He just told me what he thought of authors in general and me in particular, left me a substantial cheque for the half-year royalties and was off again. About ten minutes he was here, I believe, and he wasn't out of my sight once.'

Mr. Drizzle rubbed his chin and nodded. 'That leaves Mr. Balmer, doesn't it?' What did he want?'

Phillip smiled. 'Officially to bring me a case of whisky I'd ordered,' he said, 'but actually to beg one of my new novels. If all my reading public were as enthusiastic as Mr. Balmer, I'd be a millionaire within a couple of weeks.'

'Yes,' said Mr. Drizzle, 'I can quite believe that. How long did he stay?'

Phillip with a frown at the recollection. 'I couldn't get rid of him. About half an hour, I believe.'

'I see. And was there any opportunity for him to take the scarf, do you know?'

Phillip thought. 'Well, yes, I suppose there was if he wanted to,' he replied. 'I was out of the room for about five minutes on one occasion, I believe.'

'M'm!' murmured Mr. Drizzle. It seemed to provide the stocky man with food for thought, for he remained silent for a few seconds before he continued. 'Then what it amounts to is this: Out of the four visitors you had yesterday, two of them were in the position to get the scarf if they wanted to, and if they knew where to look for it.'

'Yes,' agreed Phillip, 'I suppose they were. But — but surely neither Mr. Balmer nor Mrs. Garvice would want to murder Margery's uncle, would they? I mean, what possible motive could they have?'

'I'm not saying that they did commit the murder, Mr. Manton,' returned the inspector. 'I'm only trying to find out who could have the opportunity to. As far as I can see, all four visitors are a wash-out — which leaves only . . . you.'

There was a silence. Margery fumbled nervously with her handkerchief and looked at Mr. Drizzle with eyes that were clouded with fear. Phillip crossed to the window and stared unseeingly into the garden.

'Yes, I suppose it does come back to me,' he admitted with a touch of bitterness. 'How it'll please Sergeant Ansell. He'd love to have arrested me this morning. Well . . . ' He looked over his shoulder. 'What are you going to do?'

The stocky man studied the situation for a few moments, then he picked up his hat, and with firm deliberation placed it on his head. 'I'm going back to Friar's Lodge,' he replied. 'I've got my car outside, and I should like you to accompany me.'

'Eh?' Phillip turned hurriedly from the window. 'Whatever for?'

'Because if we're lucky, we should find Sergeant Ansell there now. If we're not, we shall have to go to the police station, and that would be a nuisance. I shall have to put these facts before the sergeant, you know; and it would be better, I think, if you were present.'

Phillip didn't refuse. Somehow he found himself falling in ultimately with this little man's wishes. There was something about Mr. Drizzle that compelled one to acquiesce. Swiftly he locked up the house, followed Margery and Mr. Drizzle down to the car, and was soon on the way to Friar's Lodge.

It was a silent journey. Mr. Drizzle gave his whole attention to the road, and Margery sat quietly at the back. Phillip, broodingly, lapsed into a thoughtful reverie, and it was only when they began to approach the house that he seemed to come to earth again.

'Do you know,' he confided to the inspector as they swung through the gates, 'I'll bet you a pound to a penny that Ansell wants to arrest me on the spot.'

But for once he was wrong. They had scarcely got halfway up the drive when Mr. Drizzle applied his brakes with a screeching jerk. Tearing down from the house as fast as ever its condition would allow was an old, dilapidated Morris that Ansell habitually used; and at the wheel, red-faced and excited, was Ansell himself. How he stopped in time, neither Mr. Drizzle nor Phillip ever knew. But he did, and the car pulled up with a grunt. Ansell jumped out.

'Hello!' he panted. 'I was just coming to find you. I've got some news.'

'News?'

'Yes. They've just been through from Scotland Yard. They've traced that birthmark.'

'They have?' Mr. Drizzle's eyes glittered. 'What do they say?'

'Well . . . ' Ansell glanced awkwardly at Margery, who had got out of the car, but she clutched tightly at his arm.

'What's this about? What do you mean?' she asked. 'If it's something about my uncle, I want to know, no matter what it is. Do you hear?'

Mr. Drizzle signed for him to go on, and the sergeant nodded. 'Very well. I don't know what you make of it, but this is it: Records Department have only one entry concerning a birth mark shaped like a double heart. They found it in the dossier of a man called Felton Hope, who was convicted with another man for the robbery of the Hereford Diamonds about twenty years ago.'

Margery turned to the Scotland Yard man in mingled surprise and horror. 'What does this mean? You don't mean that — my uncle — ?'

Mr. Drizzle nodded.

'Then — then that accounts for it,' she said in a whisper. 'Twenty years ago . . . Oh, good heavens! No wonder they never told me!'

Mr. Drizzle nodded and turned back to Ansell. 'I thought I knew something about it,' he said. 'Where was he sent?'

'Drexford,' replied the sergeant. 'He got a sentence of ten years . . . '

His words were lost in the throaty roar of the engine as Mr. Drizzle suddenly pressed the self-starter.

'Hop out, Mr. Manton,' he said abruptly. 'This is where we part.'

The young author sprang hastily onto the gravel and looked at him in surprise. 'Where are you going?' he called as the car began to back down the drive.

'Scotland Yard,' replied the inspector. 'I want to see those records and I want to see them quick. Expect me back sometime. Goodbye.'

Ten seconds later, the car vanished swiftly through the gates, and Margery, Phillip, and Ansell were left staring after it in astonishment.

15

What the Records Revealed

It was well after five o'clock when Mr. Drizzle reached Scotland Yard. Leaving his car in the little quadrangle before the entrance to that grim building on the Thames Embankment, the stocky man nodded affably to the constable on door duty and made his way immediately up to his office. Once inside that small and cheerless apartment, he threw down his hat, lighted his pipe, and seated himself behind the big desk at which he usually worked.

After a few minutes' silent thought, he pressed the bell on his desk, and almost immediately a messenger appeared in answer to his summons. The instructions given by the inspector were brief, and approximately fifteen minutes later the officer was placing before his superior a thick wad of papers and a bulky folder.

'Records have sent everything they've got connected with the Hereford affair, sir,' he observed.

Mr. Drizzle nodded. Drawing his chair nearer the desk, he opened the folder and began to examine the contents as the officer left the room. The first thing that received his attention was a small bunch of photographs. There were half a dozen in all, depicting in various positions the likenesses of two men.

If Mr. Drizzle had ever entertained any doubts regarding the identity of Margery Trevelyn's uncle, they were dispelled now. Picking out one of the photographs, he examined it intently. It was a sharp full-face portrait taken some time back by a police photographer, and it presented in every detail the likeness of the man he knew as Matthew Trevelyn. He was younger here, of course — the printed details attached to it said thirty-two — but there was absolutely no mistaking the fine chiselled features, the large intelligent eyes, and the aristocratic curve of the rounded mouth. Matthew Trevelyn to a T. Picking up one of the reports, Mr.

Drizzle read it through. It was very short and ran thus:

* * *

'Felton Hope. Height: 5ft. 3 in. Chest: 36 in. Face: thin. Complexion: fresh. Hair: brown. Identification: Small red birth mark shaped in the form of a double heart under the left armpit. Remarks: Speaks well and writes good English. Evidently a man of education. Details: Charged on November 15th, 1912, with being instrumental in the robbery of the Hereford Diamonds. Brought up for trial with associate on November 29th, 1912. Sentenced to ten years' penal servitude on November 30th, 1912.'

* * *

The inspector next gave his attention to the other photograph. It was of a sallow-faced young man aged twenty-eight, and his name, according to the printed form, was Lew Fairlie. Mr. Drizzle looked at this for some time, and

174

as he did so he became obsessed with the idea that he had seen him before. Lew Fairlie? Lew Fairlie? The name didn't convey anything to him. Yet . . . He racked his brains desperately in an effort to put something tangible into his supposition, but for all his striving the details continued to elude him. Where, or under what circumstances, he couldn't remember, but certainly he'd seen the likeness before — yes, that was it. Perhaps the likeness. But at this point the recollection gave out.

Replacing the pictures in the folder, he went through a varied collection of press cuttings. Heavens, they had splashed it!

FAMOUS DIAMOND COLLECTION
STOLEN!
TWO MEN CAUGHT AFTER DESPERATE
CHASE THROUGH SURREY
ONE STILL AT LARGE — AND
DIAMONDS STILL MISSING
(From our Special Correspondent)

A fashionable house party, a merry throng, and festivities in full swing was the scene of one of the most daring robberies in recent years. While the guests of Lord and Lady Hereford were being entertained at Hereford Hall, Surrey, three men, who in the guise of waiters had been engaged as extras, broke into the safe and made away with the famous collection of diamonds known in Hatton Garden circles as the Hereford Collection. Fortunately the theft was discovered before the thieves had left the grounds, and the alarm was given.

A chase through Surrey ended in the early hours of this morning with two of the men being captured near Helmthorpe. The third man has disappeared completely, and it is assumed that the diamonds are with him. Police all over the country are on the lookout and it is expected that a capture will be made shortly.

It may interest our readers to know that the value of the Hereford Diamonds is estimated at something over £20,000, and . . .

Mr. Drizzle put down the paper and gazed thoughtfully across the room. £20,000! Heavens, it was a fortune. He sorted through the cuttings until he came to another that caught his eye. It ran:

HEREFORD DIAMONDS STILL
MISSING
POLICE SEARCH FOR WAITER-
BURGLAR GOES ON

While his two associates are languishing in jail, the man who escaped with the famous Hereford Diamond Collection five days ago is still at large. Despite the indefatigable efforts of police all over the country, he continues to evade their grasp. It is feared in some quarters that he may have escaped from the country, though strict surveillance has been kept on all seaports and airports.

Meanwhile, the search goes on.

★   ★   ★

Mr. Drizzle frowned and turned over the cuttings. Most of them were the same, he reflected, the only difference being that some newspapers had splashed it more than others. Then he started. A fresh report had come to light — a report that was of such a startling nature that he grasped it eagerly. The date, he noticed, was May, 1915.

DARING ESCAPE OF TWO
CONVICTS
ONE SHOT BY WARDER

What was one of the most daring prison breaks in recent years took place at His Majesty's convict prison, Drexford, last night. The convicts who escaped were Felton Hope and Lew Fairlie, the two men who were sentenced three years ago for the robbery of the celebrated Hereford Diamond Collection. How the escape was made is not yet known, but one of the convicts, Fairlie, was fired upon by a warder and fatally injured during the attempt. The other, Hope, made a complete getaway, but not until after risking recapture by staying with his dying companion.

Police are on the lookout for him, and it will assist the authorities greatly if the public will help in the search, too. We are asked, therefore, to publish a description of the wanted man, and the public are requested to notify the nearest police station immediately if they should see anyone resembling this description . . .

★   ★   ★

At this point, Mr. Drizzle put down the paper and screwed his lips in a silent whistle. So that was it? That was why Matthew Trevelyn had lived such a quiet and secluded life? Everything concerning that point came clear to him now. As an escaped convict, it was hardly likely that a man was going to place himself in the public eye, no matter how small the community in which he lived. On the contrary, he would shrink from social activities as much as possible. But — Mr. Drizzle frowned — hadn't Margery said that her uncle had only bought Friar's Lodge four years ago? In that case, where had he been before then? Abroad? It was possible. In the strife and tumult of the war years, it was possible to do anything of that nature.

Perhaps he'd joined up. Yes, that was it.

A simple disguise, and . . . what better chance when men were being accepted without question? Once abroad, he would be completely out of the grasp of British justice. And at the end of the war . . . It required little imagination to fill in the remaining years between then and now. America, Canada, France, Australia — a life of globetrotting, the accumulation of a liveable income, and then — home.

Mr. Drizzle nodded. It all seemed so simple. After all those years and under another name . . . But no. Felton Hope must have been an alias. It *must* have been, for there was Margery Trevelyn . . . Trevelyn . . . Hope . . . Of course, he'd given the name of Hope for the sake of his family. Yes, that was it. Mr. Drizzle felt very convinced.

He sighed. What a mix-up. And how on earth was he to connect it with the present case? If the other man hadn't got away with the diamonds . . . Mr. Drizzle stopped. But had he? Had he? Mr. Drizzle snapped his fingers and turned hastily to the press reports. What had it said? What had it said? Ah, here it was . . .

'*The third man has disappeared completely, and it is assumed that the diamonds are with him.*'

Assumed!

But what was there to prove that they *had* been with him? Why couldn't Trevelyn have hidden them . . . ? Or Fairlie . . . ? If the man had got away with the stones, why had nothing been heard of them? Twenty thousand pounds' worth of diamonds would take some getting rid of, and unless one had known the channels through which to pass such dangerous goods . . . Of course, it would have meant waiting for years, but by now . . .

Supposing — Mr. Drizzle closed his eyes in an expression of deep concentration — supposing they were still hidden? And supposing that Trevelyn or Fairlie had known where they were? Fairlie was dead, and that left only Trevelyn. How, then, would that account for the murder at Friar's Lodge . . . ? It wouldn't. It was equivalent to killing the goose that laid the golden egg. If Trevelyn was the only man who knew where the diamonds were, there was every reason for preserving his life.

Mr. Drizzle sighed. He felt he was groping; theorising on ideas that had nothing to back them up. If Trevelyn knew where the diamonds were, why hadn't he got them himself? Perhaps he had. Perhaps they were already through the hands of some master fence. In which case, the affair of the diamond robbery could have nothing whatever to do with this investigation.

Mr. Drizzle tapped impatiently on the desk with his fingers. Then there was the third man — he gave him this name because he knew no other. Supposing he had turned up again? How would that fit in? It wouldn't. Foolish to suggest it would. But wait a minute . . . was it? Supposing he had turned up and demanded the diamonds? And supposing Trevelyn had refused to give them to him . . . ? But no. Why should he?

Then suddenly the theory which had been unconsciously formulating within his brain presented itself, and Mr. Drizzle gasped.

Was it possible . . . ? Could it be possible . . . ?

Mr. Drizzle sat very still. Vaguely, indefinably, there came to him a theory that was so incredible that he almost discarded it. It was fantastic . . . impossible . . . but it accounted for a great many things that had seemed so insoluble. That urgent, cryptic message to Scotland Yard, the burned papers in the fire grate, and — most of all — the motive. Yes, that was it — the motive. It didn't point out the murderer, of course, but it gave him a fresh line to go on.

He smoked silently for some time, watched the shadowy dusk of the autumn evening envelope his office, and then, when the room was almost in darkness, he rose to his feet. At last, he thought he had come to something definite . . . something tangible. He gathered the scattered papers and put them back in the folder, and as he did so it suddenly dawned upon him that he was hungry — ravenously hungry. Reaching for his hat, he moved to the door. A light snack and then back to Friar's Lodge. And at Friar's Lodge . . .

Mr. Drizzle passed out of the office, his brows drawn together in a frown. Who was the third man?

16

The Man with the Hidden Face

Mr. Archie Stilman felt jubilant. Whether it was the effect of Mr. Balmer's excellent beer, or Mr. Balmer's more excellent whisky, he was not quite sure. But Mr. Stilman had had quite a liberal supply of both, and he had come to the conclusion that Mr. Balmer sold good stuff.

He felt a little hazy, it was true. The dirty tablecloth that covered the rickety table, and the cracked and broken crockery that was upon it, and all the dingy and dilapidated furniture in the evil-smelling little cottage he occupied seemed to have taken on a blurred aspect; and even the cheap oil lamp which shed its meagre and flickering light over the paper-torn walls appeared to have become curiously fogged.

But Mr. Stilman wasn't worrying. If the skies had begun to fall, Mr. Stilman wouldn't have worried. He had entered into that happy and contented state where nothing, no matter how calamitous, can every worry. He glanced blearily at the half-empty whisky bottle on the table, and decided with much regret that he felt far too tired to have even a drop more. But he wished that the infernal knocking that hammered so unmercifully into his head would cease. It was like a giant hammer. It pounded . . . pounded . . . pounded . . . and kept on pounding when he had an overwhelming desire to sleep. Yes, that was it. He'd go to sleep . . . but how could he when that confounded pounding would persist . . . ?

Then suddenly, with a jerk that almost pitched him from the chair in which he was sprawled, Mr. Stilman sat up. That pounding became a very real thing, and he realized with a start that what he had thought was a massive and particularly offensive giant hammer was nothing of the sort, but a very impatient and irritated person knocking upon his front door.

Mr. Stilman cursed in a language that was expressive of his class. He didn't want to be bothered with visitors. He wanted to sleep. Let 'em knock . . . let 'em knock . . . Perhaps they'd go away if he let 'em knock. Perhaps —

Mr. Stilman's mental conjectures came to an abrupt end. He suddenly visualized a large blue-clad figure at his door, and wondered with awful dread whether Sergeant Ansell had found out about that stolen game. Well, it was gone now. The whisky bottle was ample evidence of that. It was gone, and nobody could say where it was. And after all, if they didn't take a feller's word . . .

Mr. Stilman decided that he had better answer the front door. More by good luck than good management, he reached it without incident. In the duskiness of the tiny hallway, he had difficulty in finding the knob; but eventually, after much fumbling, he did so, and, pulling open the door, he gazed blearily into the darkness. At a first glance Mr. Stilman saw nothing, and he was about to shut the door again when a voice arrested the action.

'You needn't shut that door,' said the voice. 'I'm coming in.'

Mr. Stilman stopped, spellbound. With

eyes that were decidedly blurry, he gazed at the figure he now saw on the doorstep.

It was a man; a big, broad-shouldered man. He was clad from head to foot in a long grey raincoat, with collars that were turned up to such an extent that they almost met the drooping brim of the hat which had been pulled so well over the head. But the face . . . Mr. Stilman couldn't see the face. For one horrified moment, Mr. Stilman thought he hadn't one; then as the shock cleared his fogged brain somewhat, he realized that it was hidden; hidden beneath some black covering that was pulled tightly from head to chin. All Mr. Stilman could see were two eyes that glittered and flashed dangerously from between two narrow slits.

Mr. Stilman jumped. 'W-Wotcher want?' he asked shakily.

'You,' replied the other in a deep, rather harsh tone. He grunted contemptuously. 'I might have expected to find you like this. Result of your latest poaching exploit, I suppose. Well, are you going to keep me standing here all night?' He brushed past the startled Mr. Stilman and entered the hall. 'Shut the door; I don't want the whole of Enderby to know I'm here.'

Hastily, Mr. Stilman complied. 'There ain't much chance of that when we're on the edge of the bloomin' wood,' he observed as he followed the stranger through to the lighted parlour. 'An' who are you ter interfere, anyway?'

The stranger, who was glancing round the filthy room with obvious disgust, brought his gaze to rest upon the little poacher. 'That,' he replied slowly and deliberately, and in a tone that cut into Mr. Stilman's fuddled brain like cold steel, 'is a knowledge I should advise you not to acquire. It may be dangerous — for you.'

The little poacher clutched unsteadily at the table and gulped. 'All right,' he gasped. 'I ain't curious. But — wotcher want?'

'I told you before — you.'

'Me?' Mr. Stilman seemed to find something incredible in that statement.

'Yes. I've got a job for you. You don't suppose I should come to this disgusting hole merely for the pleasure of your company, do you?'

Mr. Stilman, protesting, flopped heavily into the chair. Mechanically he reached out for the whisky, evidently deciding that this was an occasion for further stimulation; but before his dirty fingers had time to close upon it, the bottle was whisked suddenly from his grasp.

'You'll leave that alone,' said the stranger. 'You seem to have had quite enough of that. I want you sober — see?'

It was obvious that Mr. Stilman did not see, for he regarded his visitor in an expression of befuddled amazement.

'Wotcher do that for?' he demanded indignantly. 'I'm thirsty, I am. I want a drink . . . '

The next second, Mr. Stilman experienced the peculiar sensation of being lifted bodily from his seat and shaken like a rat. Just what it was all about he didn't quite know, but by the time he had been released and pushed back forcibly into the chair, it had dawned upon his drink-sodden senses that he was dealing with a man of indisputable authority. He shook his head vigorously to disperse the mist that was already beginning to move.

'Now,' said the stranger, his words coming thickly from behind the covering mask, 'if you're quite sober, we'll get down to business. I shall pay you well for what you do, and I don't want to take any chances. Understand?'

Mr. Stilman nodded. 'All right, guv'nor. I get yer. Anythin' you say.'

'Good. Now listen. How would you like to earn twenty-five pounds?'

The little poacher looked up with a start. 'What's that you say? Twenty-five smackers?'

The man with the hidden face nodded. 'Yes. As you prefer it . . . twenty-five smackers.'

'What-ho!' Mr. Stilman, to add force to his enthusiasm, rubbed his hands briskly. 'Just try me.'

'Right.' The stranger placed his gloved hands on the edge of the table and leaned slowly forward. 'You don't like policemen, do you?'

Mr. Stilman spat viciously. 'What a question!'

'I thought you didn't. That's why I've

come to you. Well, I don't either. Policemen have a most annoying habit of poking their noses in at the most inopportune moments. This one I'm thinking of has done that now. I want him . . . removed.'

'Removed?' Mr. Stilman looked at him in surprise. 'You mean you want me ter . . . put 'im outer the way, like?'

The man in the mask nodded. 'I didn't put it so crudely, but . . . that is the idea, certainly.'

Mr. Stilman shook his head. 'Nothin' doin', guv'nor. That's an 'angin' job, that is, an' I ain't goin' ter risk my neck — not for twenty-five quid.'

The stranger breathed hard. 'I see. The price doesn't appeal to you, eh? Well, I can't afford to argue. I'll give you twenty-five now and another twenty-five when you've done your job. You'll accept those terms, or . . . '

'Or what?' asked Mr. Stilman spiritedly.

'Or perhaps you might not live to accept any other. I don't like people who are obstinate. They generally pay for it. Matthew Trevelyn was obstinate, and he paid.'

'Matthew Trevelyn?' Mr. Stilman's flabby face turned the shade of chalk. 'You mean . . . ?'

'Exactly,' said the other, nodding. 'I might not have a silk scarf handy, but there are other ways of killing a cat, you know. So what about it?'

Mr. Stilman gulped and passed a shaky hand over his forehead. Like everyone else in Enderby, his information regarding the Trevelyn affair was varied and unauthoritative. But he had heard quite enough about it to realize what a horrible, ghastly death old Trevelyn must have met with. Mr. Stilman was scared, badly scared . . .

'Wotcher want me to do?' he asked.

'Nothing,' replied the other, 'that will put that dirty neck of yours within the noose. I'm giving you fifty pounds for three seconds' work. If you're clever, you'll make a success of it. If you're not . . . well, I advise you to listen carefully.'

Mr. Stilman listened.

Ten minutes later, the man with the hidden face departed as silently as he had come, disappearing like a shadow into the fine mist of rain that had begun to fall. And in the flickering ray of the dirty oil lamp, Mr. Archie Stilman gloated greedily over twenty-five crisp pound notes.

This, decided Mr. Stilman, as he helped himself to a generous portion of whisky, was money for jam!

17

The Death Trap

With the deep, rhythmical throb of a well-tuned engine, the high-powered Bentley sped swiftly through the dripping darkness. Mr. Drizzle sat motionless, his hand resting firmly across the steering wheel, and his eyes fixed intently on the streaming road that glistened and shone in the dancing beams of the headlights. A glance at the clock on the dashboard told him that the time was nearly ten minutes to nine, and for this Mr. Drizzle was heartily thankful. Under such conditions as this, the journey from London had been anything but pleasant, and his thoughts regarding the inclemency of the weather were caustic to say the least of them.

He reached Enderby about five minutes later, and, postponing an intended call upon the loquacious Mr. Balmer, drove quickly past the Barrel Inn and through the glistening, deserted streets. Once out on the narrow road that led to Friar's Lodge, his foot pressed harder on the accelerator and he pushed the car forward at the utmost speed he dared, taking more notice of his surroundings.

The lighted macadam disappeared swiftly under the singing wheels of the car as the machine responded to his touch, and on either side of him tall trees and hedges flew past him in a bewildering blur, their bedraggled branches swaying angrily in the wind and casting weird shadows in the passing beams of the car.

A hundred yards ahead, a corner showed. The turn was sharp and the road was narrow; and, as Mr. Drizzle braked, he felt inclined to echo the sage sentiments of Mr. Balmer where the incompetence of the local highways was concerned. To any inexperienced motorist, the place was a death trap, especially on a night like this; but Mr. Drizzle, who had taken the corner before, had no qualms in negotiating it now.

Bordering it on the right-hand side was a low wooden railing, and beyond that

— blackness. A quarry it was, believed Mr. Drizzle, and he fell to wondering what chance a car would have going over that.

As he approached, the Bentley began to slow, and the rain, lashed to a sudden fury by an unexpected gust of wind, splattered madly on the windscreen, distorting completely what little vision he had of the corner.

Then it happened.

Faintly, above the hum of the engine and the thud of the rain on the roof, there came a sharp crack — and the glass of the windscreen, shattered to a thousand fragments, fell in pieces about the wheel. Something that sounded like an angry wasp whizzed past his ear. The next second there was another crack, followed almost immediately by a sudden hollow report, a loud hissing and an ominous bumping. Madly his foot jabbed the brake, and the steering wheel shuddered like a live thing in his hands as he strove to wrench it round.

With the rain beating unmercifully on his face, and the frail wooden fence shooting towards him, the car slithered across the glass like surface of the road and mounted the little grass bank. Then, with a smashing and tearing of splintered wood, it plunged through the fence; and with a roar like a thousand guns echoing in his ears, Mr. Drizzle felt himself falling . . .

In those wild, paralysing seconds that followed, Mr. Drizzle came nearer to death than he had ever been in his life. With his shoe pressing madly on the footbrake, he wrenched round the steering wheel with all the strength he could muster. The car shuddered, bumped, and came to a jolting standstill. Then, as an ominous crunching sound told him that the edge was beginning to crumble, the machine began to sway.

Too dazed to do anything but wipe the rain from his smarting face, Mr. Drizzle sat dumbly in his seat. There was a sudden awful rumble, and a large portion of the quarry edge crashed down to the depths below. The car lurched sideways, and with a smashing of broken glass, part of the fence protruded through one of the side windows, missing Mr. Drizzle's head by a mere matter of inches.

But it was this action that saved his life.

The swaying ceased, and the car, with its bonnet pointing to the black depths below, held firm.

How long he sat in that dazed, bewildered condition, Mr. Drizzle didn't know; but eventually he found himself scrambling hastily through one of the doors, and precariously back to safety.

In the drenching rain, he stood and gazed over the edge. The headlights, still on, blazed through the darkness, but even their penetrating beams failed to find the bottom. Somewhere, yards below, was a jagged floor of strewn rock, and he shuddered at the thought that he might have been down there, too.

Mr. Stilman, it seemed, had not earned his fifty pounds after all.

18

Interlude

A narrow beam of yellow sunlight was filtering into the room when Mr. Drizzle awoke the following morning. Flinging off his bedclothes, he crossed to the window and drew back the curtains. The rain, which had been falling incessantly throughout the night, had ceased, and with the coming of morning a heavy-laden sky had given way to a clear vault of sun-tinted blue, so that Mr. Drizzle looked out upon a world that was as fresh and as green as if it had been newly created. He stood for some moments by the partly open window, and as he gratefully inhaled the keen country air, it dawned upon him that he was lucky to be alive.

Was he really at Friar's Lodge? he asked himself. Was he really in a land of the living? He shuddered at the recollection of his accident last night; the long tiring walk through the pouring rain; and the exhausted, saturated condition in which he had arrived at Friar's Lodge. He ought to be dead by now. He ought to be at the bottom of the quarry with the car on top of him. Certainly he shouldn't be here, that was evident. He sighed. What Providence had saved him from such a horrible death? What stroke of luck had foiled the ingeniously made plan of his unknown antagonist? He couldn't tell; he'd never know. Perhaps it was just that he was on the side of Right and the other of Wrong. Providence usually does favour the Right.

He turned from the window and commenced to dress.

Anyway, he decided, it told him one thing. Whoever had been responsible for the ghastly, fantastic death of Matthew Trevelyn, and later for his own narrow escape, was certainly getting scared; that much was evident. And when a man got scared, he was apt to make mistakes . . .

Half an hour later, bathed, dressed, and feeling completely refreshed after his night's rest, Mr. Drizzle went down to breakfast.

A subdued clatter of crockery from the dining room told him that the morning meal was being prepared, and so, with the intention of spending the remaining few minutes on his own before the gong sounded, Mr. Drizzle made for the drawing-room.

He was glad to find that it was deserted, and further glad to find that the morning newspaper was there; but if he hoped for undisturbed solitude, his hopes were doomed to disappointment.

He had scarcely lighted his pipe and settled himself comfortably in one of the chairs when Grasset entered, and announced that Sergeant Ansell had arrived. How the butler had known where to look for him Mr. Drizzle hadn't the faintest idea, but he gave himself up to the inevitable and asked for Ansell to be shown in.

''Morning, Ansell,' he greeted as the stout sergeant was ushered into the room. 'Early-morning calls seem to have become quite a habit of yours. Anything fresh?'

'No!' Ansell shook his head and lowered his bulk into the seat Mr. Drizzle had indicated. 'I just came up to make quite sure Miss Trevelyn knew everything about the inquest.'

'M'm! It's here, isn't it! Ten o'clock this morning?'

Ansell nodded. 'That's it. But there's another thing I've come for, too. What's all this about you nearly going over the quarry last night?'

Mr. Drizzle looked up. 'Has it got to the village already?' He sighed. 'Yes, it's quite true. I nearly did go over the edge.'

Ansell frowned. 'That damned corner!' he exploded. 'I knew something like this would happen one of these days. And in weather like we had last night, too.'

'Oh, it wasn't the weather,' put in Mr. Drizzle. 'If I'd only had that to contend with, I shouldn't have minded a bit. It was something more unpleasant than that.'

'Oh?' The stout sergeant regarded him inquiringly. 'What do you mean?'

Mr. Drizzle told him.

Ansell gasped. 'A bullet?' he echoed in amazement. 'But — but — are you sure? I mean — '

Mr. Drizzle smiled. 'I've come up

against too many of them to make mistakes now,' he replied.

'But surely . . . ' Ansell was still incredulous. 'Why, it's impossible! Things like that only happen in mystery novels. Who on earth would want to — to — '

'Oh, you've no idea what an unpopular fellow I am,' replied the inspector. 'Lots of people.' He put his newspaper aside. 'But there's one person in particular just now.'

'Oh?' Ansell was never very bright. 'Who?'

'I can't tell you that — yet. But I think Matthew Trevelyn might have been able to.'

'Matthew Trevelyn? You mean — ?'

'Exactly,' said the inspector, nodding. 'The same person who killed Matthew Trevelyn. I must be getting a bit of a nuisance to him. Don't you think so?'

Ansell didn't reply. He stared thoughtfully at the stocky figure before him. 'You mean that — that you've found something out?'

Mr. Drizzle smiled and rose from his seat. 'I hadn't then. But I have now. It's a pity he tried to get rid of me.'

'Oh? Why? I mean — '

'Because it's given me my biggest clue yet,' replied Mr. Drizzle, and Ansell stared.

'How on earth do you make that out? I don't see — '

'Don't you?' Mr. Drizzle knocked out his pipe on the fire grate and proceeded to fill it again. 'Well, we'll let it go at that. It's only an idea of mine, anyway. Besides — ' He struck a match. ' — I've something else to tell you. Something I discovered at Scotland Yard. I think it's going to knock that Phillip Manton theory of yours to blazes. Are you listening?'

Ansell was. And so intent was his demeanour that Mr. Drizzle was able to impart his information without one single interruption. The expression on Ansell's face was ludicrous. To say that he was surprised would be to express it mildly. But there was more to come.

'And now I've told you that little tit-bit,' finished Mr. Drizzle, 'you can do something for me. I want you to get me an ordnance survey map; one that was issued in the year nineteen-twelve.'

Ansell stared. 'Nineteen-twelve?' he echoed. 'What do you want one of those for? We've got quite a new one at the station.'

'I don't want a new one,' returned Mr. Drizzle. 'I want one that was issued in nineteen-twelve — the year in which the Hereford Diamonds were stolen. I want a complete plan of the district — including Helmthorpe — and information concerning all houses or buildings that were empty, or in the course of construction in that year. Somewhere in this district, I believe, those diamonds were hidden. Whether they still are, I don't know. That's what I want to find out. And to do that, I must have a map that was issued at that time. So what about it?'

Ansell scratched his head. 'Well, I'll see what the Town Hall can do,' he promised. 'But if you ask me, you're looking for a needle in a haystack.'

'Maybe I am,' admitted Mr. Drizzle. 'But it's the only thing I can do at the moment, and I'm going to do it. It's better than nothing, anyway.'

And Sergeant Ansell agreed.

The inquest, which was held in the study soon after breakfast, was a dull affair. After one or two very unoriginal remarks about this being a 'bad business', the coroner opened the proceedings. They were very brief.

Doctor Westwood came first, and in long technical terms that very few of those present understood, he gave the medical evidence regarding the cause of death.

Then came Margery. She smiled slightly as Phillip Manton gave her hand a reassuring squeeze, then rose to state her evidence. With an unexpected display of calmness, she identified the body as being that of her uncle, Matthew Trevelyn, then went on to describe the manner in which she had found him. A few minutes later she sat down, and Mr. Drizzle was called.

An obvious ripple of interest ran round the pressmen and the usual quota of sightseers as Mr. Drizzle rose to take the stand, for they were all local people, and such a personage as a Scotland Yard inspector was quite a rarity among their small community. But if they had expected any sensationalism from him, they were disappointed. In his clear concise manner, the stocky man explained his association with the deceased, then stepped down again.

It was all over within half an hour. Ansell, who came next on behalf of the police, asked for and was granted the usual fortnight's adjournment, and the short proceedings broke up amid an excited chatter.

'Well, thank goodness that's over!' exclaimed Phillip Manton as he led Margery away to the drawing-room. 'But why on earth didn't they call me? Ansell was just about ready to put a rope round my neck yesterday, but now — well, he seems to have changed completely. What's it all about? He looks like a wolf that's lost its lamb. Has Mr. Drizzle anything to do with it?'

Margery nodded. 'I expect so,' she said. Briefly she explained to him what Mr. Drizzle had told her about the Records at Scotland Yard, and Phillip whistled.

'So that's it, eh? They're looking in another direction now. But if what Mr. Drizzle says about your uncle is true, how does it account for — for what's happened? I mean, if your uncle had anything to do with the — er — disappearance of the diamonds, as Mr. Drizzle seems to think he had, why should he be — be murdered?'

Margery sighed. 'I don't know. I sometimes wonder if I ever shall know. It all seems so . . . fantastic . . . unreal. But there's nothing we can do, Phillip. We've just got to leave it to Mr. Drizzle. If there's a solution he'll find it — I know he will.'

But just how near finding it Mr. Drizzle was, Margery didn't realize.

★ ★ ★

It was a quiet little party that sat down to tea that afternoon. With the funeral just over, the atmosphere which prevailed was cheerless to say the least of it, and Mr. Drizzle was inwardly thankful when Ann entered in her customary manner and informed him that he was wanted on the telephone. Wondering who on earth it could be, but nevertheless grateful for the interruption, he made his way to the hall and lifted the receiver.

'Hello? That you, Drizzle?' came an excited voice over the wire, and Mr. Drizzle recognized the now familiar tones of Sergeant Ansell. 'Listen, I've got some news for you. You remember that scrap of postcard Grasset picked up on the night of the murder? Well, we've traced it!'

'You have?' Mr. Drizzle's eyes glittered. 'That's splendid. And what's the result?'

'Surprising!' chuckled Ansell. 'As surprising as your information from Scotland Yard. Do you know what those letters 'H-A-R-M-' stood for? You'd never guess. Harmsworth's Brewery, Helmthorpe. It's part of what they call a traveller's advice card, I believe.'

'Well?'

'Don't you see?' asked Ansell. 'Why, it's as plain as a pikestaff! I got through to the brewery this afternoon and they told me that they usually send those things to innkeepers when their traveller is about to call on them. But that's not all. They told me something else, too. They told me that there's only one place where they send them to here. The address is 'The Barrel Inn, Enderby'. And that means — '

' . . . that the man on the terrace should have been Mr. Joshua Balmer,' finished Mr. Drizzle. He gasped. 'Are you sure . . . absolutely certain . . . ?'

'Of course I am,' retorted Ansell. 'I don't see how it could be anybody else. But you sound disappointed. What's the matter?'

'Nothing,' replied Mr. Drizzle. 'Only it means that if what you say is true, I've got to scrap my theory, that's all.'

And Grasset, descending the stairs, heard Mr. Drizzle replace the receiver with a clatter.

19

Mr. Balmer Gets a Shock

Joshua Balmer shot home the heavy wooden bolt and turned the massive iron key as the shambling footsteps of his final customers died faintly down the street. Giving the handle of the door one vigorous pull as if to ascertain whether his precautionary efforts had been successful, he walked slowly back to the bar-parlour.

Two of the ancient oil lamps that illuminated the place had been turned out, and only one near the fireplace remained lighted. Walking over to the hearth, he dropped into the high-backed chair which, in opening hours, was usually occupied by the local church-warden. He sat for a few moments gazing unseeingly into the dying embers of the fire, and his large brow creased in numerous frowns.

Mr. Balmer was puzzled and considerably worried, and he found it exceedingly difficult to make up his mind. His hand strayed slowly to the inside of his jacket and almost unconsciously, from some inner recess, he extracted a small thin envelope. At one time its colour had been white, but its continual presence in Mr. Balmer's pocket had now reduced it to a doubtful state of dirty grey. He turned it over and over, held it up wonderingly to the yellow light of the oil lamp, and sighed.

As a keen student of detective stories, Mr. Balmer was well aware that this might contain the very clue the police were looking for; but in the true manner of human nature, he possessed a selfish regard for his own personal well-being, and knew full well that if he handed it over to the police, it was quite likely that his long cherished ambition of seeing the inside of a prison cell would be realized in a manner he would not appreciate.

A sudden gust of wind down the cavernous chimney stirred the embers in a shower of sparks and the fire blazed fitfully. Mr. Balmer shivered. Storm blowing up, he reckoned; a heavy storm, too.

He looked at the envelope and frowned. What on earth was he to do with the thing? he asked himself. What on earth *could* he do? He wished to goodness he'd never seen it — wished to goodness he'd never been near Friar's Lodge. Supposing they found out? Supposing they discovered that the man on the terrace had been him? Of course they'd think he was the murderer — they were bound to.

Mr. Balmer swallowed hard. They'd never believe him — never. Once they'd made a capture, they'd never let him go. He knew the police. And this thing. This made it worse. What was in it? What did it contain? He couldn't tell. He couldn't even imagine. Perhaps it was nothing important after all. Perhaps . . . But what had it been doing on the terrace?

He suddenly found that in his explorations, his thumb had become wedged beneath the top corner of the flap. He moved it to take it out, and as he did so the flap began to lift. Queer! Rotten gum, he decided. Or perhaps it had got too dry on account of it being in his pocket so much. Anyway, it didn't stick.

Then . . .

Why shouldn't he? he asked himself.

He looked over his shoulder and peered into the shadowy depths of the room. There was nobody there he knew. But all the same . . . Suddenly he made up his mind, and without doing any noticeable damage to the envelope, he opened it. After all, he'd found it, and he ought to know what was in it.

His trembling fingers fumbled inside the little packet, and he withdrew a small piece of notepaper. Expensive, he reckoned — very expensive; he could see before he opened it that the address was embossed. Running a quivering tongue over his parched lips, he unfolded the paper. It was covered from top to bottom with small neat handwriting, and Mr. Balmer stared.

Well, he'd opened it now, so he might as well read it . . .

Mr. Balmer did.

'Lord!' he exclaimed suddenly. 'Lord!'

He stared at that small sheet of paper as if it had been alive. What was it he had discovered? What horrible secret had he stumbled upon? His popping eyes ran swiftly over the words and his brain tried valiantly to assimilate their meaning. Diamonds . . . diamonds . . .

He gulped and passed a shaking hand over his perspiring brow. What did it all mean? What was it all about? Diamonds? Diamonds? What had diamonds to do with it?

He calmed himself. There was nothing to get worked up about. Nothing to worry about. He'd read it through again. Yes, that was it. Read it through again. Perhaps he'd understand it better then . . .

He lifted the paper nearer the light to make sure of seeing every detail.

'Lord!' exclaimed Mr. Balmer a few second later, as he let the paper fall to his knee. 'Oh my Lord!'

He stared for some moments at the dancing flames of the fire as they cast weird and grotesque patterns on the shadowy ceiling. A sudden gust of wind blew a cloud of acrid smoke into the room, and the flame of the oil lamp flickered unsteadily.

'Diamonds!' muttered Mr. Balmer in an awed sort of tone. 'Twenty thousand pounds' worth — and within a stone's throw. Lord!'

The startling nature of his discovery had unnerved him, and he felt a queer trembling sensation in the pit of his stomach. He sat for a few minutes, deadly still. A furious splatter on the window panes marked the advent of rain, but Mr. Balmer didn't hear it. The ancient signboard at the front of the building began to creak as it swayed in the grip of the rising wind; somewhere at the back a loose shutter banged intermittently; and a great hollow roaring sound filled the chimney like some invisible monster of the storm. But the sounds of the gale passed unheeded.

How long he sat in that statue-like position, Mr. Balmer didn't know, but finally he roused himself and glanced quickly round the room. It was deserted. The short little bar was shrouded in a world of shadows, and a tall pile of tumblers stacked precariously at one end reflected in shimmering concord the leaping tongues of the fire. He listened, and above the ceaseless clamour of the rain on the window, and the choking gurgling of the fall-pipe outside the door, the great-grandfather clock which was hidden in the farthest corner of the room began to strike. What was it? . . . eight . . . nine . . . ten . . . eleven . . . Yes, that was it. Eleven.

He stuffed the paper suddenly into his pocket and rose to his feet. A trifle unsteadily, he walked over to the bar. A half-empty whisky bottle was standing near the pile of tumblers, and, seizing it, he splashed out himself a generous portion.

With a trembling hand, he raised the glass to his lips and was just about to swallow it whole when sudden furious knocking on the door of the bar-parlour made him start violently. Half the contents of the glass splashed over his jacket.

Mr. Balmer turned, white-faced. For some moments he stood perfectly still, listening only to the hiss of the falling rain and the low rumble of approaching thunder. Who on earth could be knocking on his door at this time of night? Who on earth would want to be out in this sort of weather? Who —

The knocking came again, heavier, louder, and more insistent than ever.

Mr. Balmer gulped. He replaced the glass on the counter and glanced over in the direction of the door. He shuddered. He'd locked that door for the night and he wasn't too keen about opening it again.

Slowly, reluctantly, he moved across the sanded floor. The knocking came again, impatient, urgent.

'All right,' he called, 'I'm coming.'

The sound of his own voice reassured him a little, and he hastened to the door and drew back the bolt. He turned the cold iron key and opened the door a fraction.

'What d'yer want?' he asked as he poked his head through the aperture. 'Who is it?'

The only answer he received was an unpleasant shower of drenching rain as the wind drove it inwards. Mr. Balmer spluttered and opened the door wider — and the next second he received the biggest shock of his life. For standing on the doorstep, shadowy and indistinct, was the man with the hidden face.

Mr. Balmer gasped.

Momentarily overwhelmed by the suddenness of the situation, the innkeeper felt stunned. He backed instinctively as the big man entered the bar-parlour and gazed incomprehensively at the sudden shower of water that was shed over the sanded floor. He watched, as though in a dream, the figure carefully close the door and shot back the bolt. He vaguely felt himself being pushed back into the room; and it was only when the man began to speak that he became aware that he possessed any faculties at all.

'Mr. Balmer, I believe?' said the figure.

Mr. Balmer nodded.

'Gentleman who was on the terrace at Friar's Lodge a few nights ago?'

Mr. Balmer jumped.

'Come now, you're not denying that fact?'

Mr. Balmer was incapable of denying anything.

The other shrugged. 'I see, Mr. Balmer,' he went on, 'that you persist in maintaining a somewhat aggravating silence. It appears that my presence here affords you some slight discomfort. Well, believe me, I don't intend to stay long.'

Mr. Balmer was grateful. In some inexplicable manner, he was able to find his voice. 'What — what d'yer want?' he stammered.

'Something which I believe is in your possession,' said the other. 'And as soon as I get it, I intend to go. So it's up to you. I see you don't like my company, and I'm not particularly keen on yours.' The black covering which hid his face flapped slightly as he drew a deep breath. 'I'm not going to waste time on trivialities. I'll come straight to the point. I want the envelope you picked up on the terrace the night Matthew Trevelyn was murdered.'

'Envelope?' echoed Mr. Balmer in such complete surprise that it sounded almost convincing.

'Envelope,' agreed the other. 'And you needn't say you haven't got it.'

'But — but I 'aven't,' said Mr. Balmer. It seemed that such an answer was expected of him. 'I don't know what yer talking about.'

The other's hand moved restlessly in the pocket of his large raincoat. 'Mr.

Balmer, I have very little patience. This toy is intended to oppose any line of resistance you may be foolish enough to attempt. I want that envelope — quickly.'

Mr. Balmer's staring eyes looked at the object clutched between the curling fingers as the other withdrew his gloved hand. It was a neat little revolver — small, black, and deadly. Mr. Balmer's contemplated resistance wavered.

'I don't know what yer mean,' he stammered, his brow feeling damp and clammy under the rising beads of perspiration. 'I ain't got no envelope, nor never 'ad.'

'No?' The other nodded his head across the room. 'Your intelligence, Mr. Balmer, is astounding — or perhaps I have been misinformed. I have always been under the impression that they were called envelopes.'

The innkeeper slowly followed the other's gaze. Close by the seat in which he had been sitting was the envelope he had found at Friar's Lodge, crumpled and empty. He groaned. He hadn't noticed it when it had fallen from his knee. He looked up.

'Well?' The other's eyes glistened

menacingly from between two narrow slits. 'What have you to say now? It's a pity you were misguided enough to open it — a great pity indeed.' His demeanour suddenly changed and he threw off all vestige of banter. 'Where are the contents of that envelope? Quick. I haven't time to waste.'

'I don't know what yer mean,' protested Mr. Balmer. 'I ain't 'ad no envelope. An' as for any contents — '

The man with the hidden face cursed. 'Do you want a bullet in your fat carcass?' he rasped angrily. 'Do you want me to drop you where you stand? Hand over what you found in that envelope — now.'

Mr. Balmer started back, stung. Those eyes — they were staring at him, and they were wild and bright. The fingers were clutched tightly round the butt of the revolver, and there was a deadly purpose in the cold, harsh voice. Mr. Balmer backed before the other's advance. Somewhere on the counter was that whisky bottle. At least he'd have a sporting chance . . .

'Well, what about it? Are you going to hand it over?'

'I can't,' gasped Mr. Balmer tearfully. 'I ain't got no envelope. Don't I keep on tellin' yer? I don't know what yer talking about.'

The fingers tightened on the revolver. Mr. Balmer blanched. He just wanted time, only a little time . . . He felt the rim of the counter press into the middle of his back. His fingers fumbled behind him and came in contact with the cold, round bottle. It was the most comforting thing he'd ever felt. The figure before him advanced.

'I'm waiting,' he said. 'What about it? Or do you want me to look for it?'

Mr. Balmer grasped hold of the bottle neck. He watched the other intently; the wide-brimmed hat pulled low over the glittering eyes; the constant movement of the silken face covering as he drew quick short breaths; and the threatening, menacing movement of the black-nosed revolver. Then, with a cry of rage, the man with the hidden face launched himself forward, and the innkeeper swung his weapon round.

'Put it down,' screamed the other as he realized Mr. Balmer's frenzied intentions.

'Put it down, I tell you. If you don't — '

His words were lost in the sudden crack of the revolver. Mr. Balmer felt a sharp stinging pain somewhere near his head; heard through the deafening roar that filled his ears a smash of broken glass as the bottle was dashed to fragments on the opposite wall; and then, as everything went black before his eyes, he slipped with a groan to the floor.

20

The Motive

The tiny kitchen of Briar Cottage was silent and deserted when the man with the hidden face switched on the light. Peeling off his soaking raincoat, he threw it over a chair, then commenced to unfasten the tapes of his essential face covering. There was no need to endure its discomforts here, he reflected, as he placed it on the table together with his hat and gloves. Not for this job, anyway.

He crossed over to a cupboard and opened the door, and after a few minutes' searching he eventually found a candlestick. With fingers that trembled with excitement as he fumbled for a match, he lighted the candle, then walked through to the passage.

Outside, the wind rose in steady cadence as the storm continued, and the guttering flame of the candle flickered perilously as he opened the cellar door under the back of the stairs. A cool wave of damp air met him as he descended the spider-webbed steps, and he found that it was necessary to shield the candle with his hand to prevent it from being blown out.

Once at the bottom, he paused and looked round. A huge mountain of coal occupied quite a considerable space at the opposite end, and numerous tool boxes littered the floor at frequent intervals.

Setting the candle on the top of an upturned box near the steps, he fumbled in his pocket for the paper he had found on the inquisitive Mr. Balmer.

He laughed. Fancy! In this cellar of all places. Here, where he could have got time and time again — and he had never known. It was ironical.

Holding the paper near the light, he unfolded it and began to examine the contents again. How many had it said? Fifteen? He glanced down at the floor and made a series of rapid calculations. Composed of large stone flags, the floor was hidden beneath an age-old film of grime and coal-dust, but it was still possible to make out where each one ended and the other began.

Starting from the lowest stone of the cellar steps, he moved slowly across the floor, counting as he went . . . Eleven . . . twelve . . . thirteen . . . fourteen . . .

'Damn!' he exclaimed suddenly.

The fifteenth flag lay directly under the massive heap of coal.

He stood for a few moments, nonplussed. The question was, what was he going to do? The hour was late, and — His eyes caught sight of the heavy coal shovel and he made up his mind. There was only one thing he *could* do. And after all, there was nobody to hear him . . .

He grasped hold of the shovel and began shifting the coal as fast as he could. The job was no light one, and large beads of perspiration, stood on his brow as he laboured at his self-imposed task. In the confined space of the cellar the noise was deafening, and it drowned for a time even the din of the storm.

But his task was worthwhile. In a few minutes or so he had moved all the coal which had been covering the flagstone, and with a glitter of excitement in his eyes, he flung down the shovel and scrutinised the ground intently.

Yes, this was it.

He lifted the candle across the cellar and placed it on the floor, and after examining the contents of the largest tool chest, he found a crowbar and began to scrape along the edge of the flagstone.

How long he worked he didn't know, but his temples throbbed like a steam hammer as he tried to lift the stone from its bed. Encrusted with years of coal dirt and firmly embedded by the weight of the coal, it was difficult, but finally he was able to insert the thin edge of the crowbar along the narrow edge of the stone.

Exerting all his strength, he pulled, but the stone refused to move. With increased vigour he worked on, the howl of the wind and the rumble of the thunder drowning the monotonous scrape of the crowbar.

Hot, clammy, and tired from his unusual exertions, he took off his coat and flung it on the damp ground. His arms ached terribly, but he refused to relax for one moment.

Minutes passed — minutes that seemed like a lifetime. The candle flickered and diminished in size as each drop of grease trickled slowly into the candlestick. Then, with a sudden and unexpected crunching sound, he discovered that the flag would lift a little. He prised, and now that it had been loosened somewhat, the stone came up with surprising ease and fell with a terrific crash on to the adjoining flag-stones.

He dropped the crowbar and fell to his knees. Undisturbed for years, the ground was as hard as the stone itself. With perspiration running down his face in glistening streams, he grabbed hold of the small trowel he had brought from the tool box and began to dig feverishly into the earth.

His fingers were sore and his nails were broken, but he was unconscious of any physical discomfort. His eyes, glinting wildly, watched the earth as he turned it under the trowel, then suddenly he gasped aloud as the steel instrument scraped against something hard. Panting madly, he dug the earth around it, and in a few minutes he had disclosed the dirt-encrusted form of an oblong-shaped box.

'I've found it!' he cried hoarsely. 'I've found it!'

With trembling fingers he picked out the box and examined it. Made of steel and very heavy, it had once had a polish like gloss, but now it shone dully in the feeble yellow light — dirty, grey and tarnished.

Panting with excitement, he fingered the lid, and found to his uncontrollable joy that it lifted.

He gasped. Startled, spellbound and oblivious to any outside element, he stared at what he saw.

Nestling softly in a snug red cushion which the dampness of years had marked only slightly were twenty dazzling diamonds, all of which winked at him with a hundred twinkling eyes as they reflected the flickering light of the candle. He gazed at them in breathless admiration, unable for a few moments to utter a single word.

Then: 'At last,' he muttered. 'At last.'

He fingered each stone tenderly,

caressed their smooth proportions; and the thrill of their touch seemed to fill him with a new and relentless determination. With his face contorted in such a mask of greed and evil satisfaction that it would have been completely unrecognizable to those who knew him so well, he replaced them carefully in the box and rose to his feet.

At last they were his — at last, after months of careful planning and striving. At last in spite of all the dangers and obstacles and dangers that had barred his way.

He smiled. There was only one thing now. Only one more scene. And that scene was to be, played at Friar's Lodge — tonight.

21

Margery Trevelyn's Ordeal

Margery Trevelyn woke with a start.

For some seconds she lay staring into the darkness of her room, her heart thumping wildly with a strange, unaccountable sense of fear. She listened, but only the sound of the rain rattling on her window-panes and the furious gurgle of the fall-pipe outside her window came to her straining ears. She gasped. What on earth had made her wake so suddenly? she asked herself. And what was the reason for the unpleasant feeling of dampness on her forehead?

She raised herself slowly on one elbow. Was it the storm; the howl of the wind as it tore unmercifully at the unprotected bulk of Friar's Lodge? Or was it the sudden, tremendous crashes of thunder that shook the very house itself? She shook her head. She'd slept in worse storms than this without waking, and she considered herself impervious to such disturbances now. Then — what was it?

She turned over to the left side to take a look at her wristwatch, but she found that for some mysterious reason its luminous dial was no longer visible. She frowned. Funny! She was certain she'd left it on her night table before getting into bed. But . . . she couldn't see the table either — not even a faint, indistinct outline. She passed her tongue over her quivering lips and was surprised to find that they were unusually dry. Queer! She stared intently at the surrounding darkness that confronted her piercing eyes. Gradually the other objects in the room began to distinguish themselves as her eyes became more accustomed to the gloom; the smooth, curved top of the bed rail; and the slim form of her dressing-gown just as she had slung it over. She turned her eyes to the table again — then realized with a start what had obstructed her vision.

Silent and motionless, a tall, overpowering figure was standing by the side of her bed. She gasped in horror and clutched involuntarily at her throat.

'I shouldn't make a noise if I were you,' said a low, harsh voice in her ear. 'I shouldn't try screaming.'

She opened her mouth, but a huge damp hand choked the cry of terror that was born in her throat. She struggled to wrench it aside, but a strong and terrible grip round her shoulders defeated any such attempt. She bit deep into the hand that covered her mouth, but the action only damaged her teeth as they sank into the tough, evil-smelling leather of damp gloves.

'I warned you not to scream,' said the voice. 'It won't do you any good.'

She choked and struggled vainly in the iron grip that held her, but the other only chuckled.

'If you're sensible, you'll save yourself heaps of trouble,' he went on. 'I want you to get up and dress.'

Margery shook her head and mumbled something unintelligible.

'I think you will,' said the other. 'Now.'

He threw the bedclothes aside in a heap and lifted her bodily to the floor.

'Now,' he said as she seemed half stunned and motionless with fear. 'Get dressed. I've got a revolver in my hand, and though it's very difficult to see you, I warn you that I shan't hesitate to use it — even on you, my dear.'

Mechanically, her eyes dilated with fear, she reached for her clothes. With that grim shadowy figure standing over her, she dressed as well as her trembling fingers and the awful semi-darkness would allow. Her frock — she knew she had got it on back to front over her night apparel; her stockings — she had an idea they were inside out; and her shoes, all encased her trembling limbs within the space of three minutes or less.

'All right,' said the voice when she told him she was dressed. 'Now you can get a hat and coat and then we're ready.'

Horrified, half fainting, she moved over to the wardrobe and slipped on the first coat she came to. With her hair scattered all over her head, she put on a hat and waited.

'Good,' said the voice. 'I think that will do. Come on.'

'Where — where are we going?' she ventured.

'That doesn't matter yet, my dear,' whispered the voice, and she felt a hand on her arm. 'You'll know that presently. At the moment, we're leaving Friar's Lodge. And you'd better not make a sound.'

Silently they crossed the room and came to the door, and like veritable shadows they passed on to the landing beyond. A dazzling flash of lightning from one of the windows over the stairs lit the corridor from end to end, and Margery glanced speculatively at the room next to hers. Mr. Drizzle was in there, and if she could only —

He must have read her thoughts, for she suddenly felt a small hard shape dig into her back.

'You'll be sorry if you do,' he whispered. 'I've got this thing silenced and no one would hear a sound. Get going.'

Reluctantly, with all vestige of hope dying in her breast, she was propelled along the landing and down the stairs. The grip on her arm never relaxed for one second, and that small hard pressure

236

in her back constituted a menace she knew she could not defy. They reached the front door a few minutes later, and, after he had drawn the bolt, they stepped out into the porch. The rain was coming down in torrents, and she could even feel the splatter of it as they stood on the steps.

'It's a bit wet,' he observed, 'but that's all the better. I should put your collar up if I were you. We've a little walk before us.'

Mechanically she obeyed his order, and with his hand still gripping her arm, they crunched their way down the soggy drive. She gasped breathlessly as the rain stung her face, and it took her all her time to realize that this was a grim reality and not some fantastic nightmare. The sodden pebbles crunched repulsively and got into her shoes as she stumbled over them, and her feet felt icy cold as her stockings became saturated. A sudden crack of thunder made her start violently, and she staggered.

'I can't go on,' she gasped. 'Oh *please* let me go.'

Two steady hands helped her to her feet. 'There's not much further to go,' he said. 'I'm not going to lose you now, my dear.'

She realized that his grasp had relaxed a little, and with a wild, desperate wrench she dragged herself free.

'Come back!' he called. 'Damn you, come back!'

With her heart pounding, she plunged into the dripping darkness of the night. Her sense of direction was completely gone, but the one thought in her mind was to put as much distance as she could between her and her antagonist. The stumbling, running footfalls behind her told her that he was close at hand, and she put on a last desperate spurt. Her foot caught against something hard, and with a choking cry she fell headlong to the ground. She realized bitterly that she had stumbled over the edge of the drive, but the knowledge was of little use to her now. She felt herself dragged roughly to her feet, and a fierce hand dug into her arm.

'Damn you!' hissed an angry voice in her ear. 'If you do that again, I'll shoot you. I swear it. Come on.'

Panting, despairing, she staggered on, and after what seemed an age they came to the bottom of the drive. A dull throbbing and a dim reflection of light told her that he had a car waiting, and she was at least thankful that they had not to continue their journey on foot, wherever it was to lead her.

All hope of escape had now sapped from her, and she allowed herself to be pulled to the car without any resistance. At least she would get out of the rain. Vaguely she saw him wrench open the door, then she felt herself pushed inside. She sank into the seat with a deep breath of exhaustion — then realized a fact that filled her with a horror indescribable even to herself.

The car — it was Phillip's . . . She stared in horror at the familiar interior . . . Phillip's car. A cold wave of mental agony swept over her as she watched the figure clamber into the seat beside her. Phillip's car . . . and the driver . . . ?

'Who are you?' she gasped suddenly. 'Where are you taking me?'

The other's words were lost in the roar of the engine, and he turned a terrifying masked face towards her. She clutched desperately at his arm as the car began to move through the night.

'Who are you, I say? What are you doing in this car?'

A low, sibilant chuckle came to her ears. 'Driving it, my dear. Driving it away to a place of happiness — for both of us.'

She shuddered. 'You're not . . . Phillip?'

The chuckle came again. 'You'd like to know, wouldn't you?' He shook his head. 'No, I'm not Phillip. From tonight — from the moment I get back to Briar Cottage — Phillip Manton will only be a name. Phillip Manton won't exist anymore. And after all, one name's just as good as another.' He paused calculatingly. 'I shall have to change my name, of course. Let's see . . . a nice, respectable name like — like Brown. Or perhaps Jackson. Anyway, whatever it is, you'll get used to it. You'll have to — as my wife.'

'Wife?'

'Yes. We're going to be married. That's

why I'm taking you away. Margery, I love you. I have done ever since I entered this business. I came to Enderby with only one intention — to find the diamonds. Well, I've found them — and I've found a wife also.'

The voice came to her from a distance. She clutched at the seat in a desperate effort to hold her slipping senses.

'You don't think I shall ever . . . marry you?'

'Why not? I've always wanted to marry you.'

'Oh, you're mad — hopelessly mad!'

'Am I?' He turned that awful shapeless mask towards her again. 'Is it madness to want to marry the only woman you've ever loved?' He laughed; a harsh, bitter sound. 'You poor creature! You don't know what you're getting. Why, I'm the richest man you've ever met — or likely to meet. Look.'

He took one hand from the steering wheel and fished about in his pocket. She watched him with a queer sort of stupefied wonder as he pulled out a small oblong box and opened it.

'Look! There's my fortune. Look!'

She stared in sheer amazement. The diamonds sparkled and glittered in the feeble light from the dashboard as he pushed them into her hands.

'Look at them. Hold them. That's what's going to make you rich, my dear. Richer than you've ever been in your life. Look at them — go on!'

She took the box in a dream, her eyes staring in bewilderment. To her they were just stones, beautiful perhaps, but just mere stones; but she knew that to him they represented all he had worked for. Slowly, dreadfully slowly it seemed to her, an idea slid into her numbed brain, and she glanced quickly round her. The window next to her was open slightly at the top; she could feel the draught of it. With a speed she would have never believed possible in her condition, she snapped shut the lid of the box, at the same time lowering the window as fast as her fingers could turn the handle. He looked at her in surprise as he felt the sudden unaccountable draught,; and the next second, before he had time to realize what she was doing, she had flung the box out of the window.

He stamped furiously on the brake, and the car lurched wildly as it screamed to a standstill. A torrent of horrifying curses tumbled from his lips.

'Damn you! By God, I'll make you pay for that! I'll make you pay!'

A sudden stab of light that cut through the solid darkness told her he'd had a torch in his pocket. Held roughly in an iron grip, she was dragged forcibly along the road, the beam of the torch flashing to the left and right.

'Let me go!' she cried. 'Let me go!'

'I'll let you go,' he promised. 'Let you go to hell if you've lost those stones. I'll make you wish you'd never been born. Make you scream for mercy! Make you rather have all the devils of hell at your heels . . . '

She was dragged roughly through the drenching rain, his torch flashing from one side to the other as he searched for the missing box containing the diamonds. A few yards further on they found it, but the box had sprung open and half a dozen stones were lying on the road.

Forgetful, oblivious for the moment to anything but the jewels, he dropped to his knees with a cry of horror.

'Oh my God! If you've lost any . . . If you've lost any . . . ' She realized suddenly that he was no longer holding her, and like a flash she darted off into the darkness.

'Come back!' he screamed. 'Come back or I'll shoot. I'll shoot, I tell you!'

Madly, with the rain stinging her face like a whiplash, she ran on. She slithered and tripped over the wet macadam till she felt she must surely fall, but the fear in her heart lent her wings. One predominant thought ran through her brain. She mustn't be caught . . . she mustn't be caught . . . She said it over and over again till the words formed a rhythm that fitted identically with the furious pad-pad of her feet.

. . . Mustn't be caught . . . mustn't be caught . . . The sound seemed to fill her head till she felt it must burst — and she knew that unless some miracle undreamed of happened, she would be. For the running footsteps and the harsh laboured breathing behind her told her that.

And then, when she thought that all hope of salvation was lost, Fate in its mercy intervened on her behalf.

She heard a sudden awful thud and a stream of angry curses as the man with the hidden face measured his length on the roadway, and the next moment a bright light in the distance heralded the approach of a car.

She saw the light racing towards her with the speed of an express train; saw the car draw up with a jerk only a matter of inches from her; and as she recognized the startled, surprised features of Mr. Drizzle behind the wheel, all her senses left her and she slipped to the roadway in a faint.

22

Behind the Mask

A series of low, disturbing rumbles, sudden unaccountable flashes of light, and a ghastly throbbing pain in his head that made him feel horribly sick.

Phillip Manton awoke to the realities of life to the accompaniment of these several distinct and unpleasant sensations.

For some seconds he lay perfectly still, striving desperately to understand the reason for the terrible throbbing in his head, until at last, failing to do so, he opened his eyes with a groan. His first impression upon surveying the blank and colourless world above him was that he must be in the throes of some weird and unusual nightmare, but as a dazzling flash of lightning through the uncurtained window of his bedroom lit the place from end to end, he realized with a start that he was fully awake — and in bed.

With a jerk he tried to sit up, but a curious restriction to his limbs rendered the movement impossible, and it suddenly dawned on him that his hands were tied behind his back.

He frowned. Tied behind his back? What on earth had been happening to him? Why was he trussed up like this?

A flood of memory came surging back to him. Of course. The figure in the bedroom; that repulsive, black face that moved over the flicker of lightning; and the revolver. Yes, that was it. It was the revolver that had hit him.

He grunted. And what was the reason for *this* attack? The second within a few days. What was there about him that seemed so unpopular? And who in the name of Goodness was his attacker?

He groaned and turned awkwardly on the other side. The pain in his head was easing a little, and the violent sickness was beginning to settle somewhat.

He heard the rain patter furiously against the window and could see in the recrudescent flashes of lightning the water streaming down in torrents. What a beastly night, he reflected. Night? Was it night? he asked himself. Surely it must be the small hours of morning by now . . . He tried to look at the little clock on the table by the side of his bed, but save for a dim grey blur, he was unable to make out anything.

He bit his lip. Well, what was he going to do? He didn't relish the idea of staying like this all night. He pulled hard at the ropes that held his hands, but the effort made no impression. He fumbled clumsily with the huge knot that dug so painfully into his wrist, then realized after a moment or two that he wasn't bound with rope, after all. It was the silken cord from his dressing-gown! He laughed. Well, if that didn't beat everything — oh well, it was no use tugging about like this. Nothing short of a knife could free his hands now.

He pondered some moments on what he should do next. Until Mrs. Gribbs arrived in the morning, there seemed to be nothing he could do. Phillip smiled in the darkness. Poor Mrs. Gribbs. What a shock she was in for this time. He wondered how she would get into the house. Perhaps she'd have to climb through the window again — that was, if the unknown marauder had entered by the window. Anyway, he could shout to tell her to break the back door in: there was an axe in the garage.

He sighed. In any case, he couldn't get free until morning. So what was the good of bothering? He might just as well go to sleep — if the storm would let him. In fact . . .

He listened.

Faintly, above the din of the storm, sounded the insistent throbbing of a motor engine that grew louder and louder as it drew nearer. Coming this way, thought Phillip, and — He caught his breath. Surely . . . If that wasn't his car — But no! It was impossible. How could it be?

Yet . . . It was his car — he *knew* it was; and his conviction became more pronounced as he heard it pull up before the cottage. Who on earth?

He listened intently as he heard the familiar slam of the door; recognized the squeak of his garden gate; and distinguished the sound of footsteps on the garden path. Someone was coming up to the house — and it needed little or no imagination to tell him that it must be his previous visitor.

A muffled thud that floated up from below informed him that whoever it was had entered by the front door, and he heard the sound of footsteps in the hallway. He tensed a little as a gentle creak announced that someone was ascending the stairs — three at a time. He knew that, because the stairs never made a sound if you came up singly; but if you took more than one they generally creaked. Extra pressure, he supposed. Anyway, it was obviously someone who felt pretty sure of himself. Otherwise he would never have come up like that.

Phillip stiffened as the knob of his door rattled, and, glancing across the room, he dimly made out a moving bulk as the door opened.

Now for it.

He lay still — deadly still, hardly daring to breathe as a shadowy figure approached the bedside. Phillip closed his eyes and feigned sleep. A quick, laboured panting told him that the man had been hurrying, and Phillip wondered why. A silly thing to wonder, because in a few minutes it wouldn't matter what the cause had been; he wouldn't be alive to care. The dull glint of a revolver through his half-closed eyes and the metallic click of the safety catch told him that.

The figure bent slowly over him, and Phillip heard a harsh chuckling in his ear.

'Pity you're still asleep, my friend. I must have hit you harder than I expected. Still — ' He sighed. ' — it can't be helped. I'd like to wake you up, but I haven't time. Goodbye. This is where we part.'

Another spasm of chuckling told Phillip that he was due for the end any second now, and he decided that it was time he took a hand — if he could. Or perhaps feet would be better . . . ? Yes, perhaps they would . . .

He suddenly brought his two feet together, and with all his might he launched out at the figure by the side of him. There was a sudden choking gasp, and the figure went toppling over into the room.

'One for you, old man!' gasped Phillip

breathlessly, then added to himself: 'But how on earth I'm going to get out of this mess, I don't know.'

A stream of angry curses came from behind the other's mask as he scrambled to his feet and sought for his revolver. 'Curse you!' he snarled. 'I'll kill you for that!'

Phillip turned over and over and fell off the bed at the other side. He landed with a bump that sent his head throbbing again, but he smiled. Quite an unexpected move, he reflected.

The next second he paled. There was a sudden dull plop, a stab of yellow flame, and something went whizzing past his ear. Phillip groaned. There didn't seem to be much chance now. He rolled over and over as a fusillade of shots thudded into the floor only a matter of inches from him.

The figure darted round the end of the bed, intent on getting at closer quarters. Phillip's foot caught against the spindle of a chair and he kicked out with all his might. The chair went thudding over in the darkness, and the next second there was a terrific crash as the unknown attacker fell headlong over it.

Phillip rolled to the far corner of the room. His head felt battered to pieces and on the point of bursting. He couldn't keep this up much longer. A jagged ribbon of lightning flickered across the sky, and in that brief instant Phillip saw the shadowy bulk of the figure as he came to his feet; he heard him kick the chair angrily aside; saw him stoop and pick up the revolver again; and saw him slowly approach. There was a deadly, relentless purpose in the movement, and in another streak of lightning Phillip saw a gloved finger tighten firmly round the trigger.

Phillip closed his eyes.

The next second he opened them again, as the room became filled with a blinding shower of lights, and for one horrified moment Phillip thought that the cottage must have been struck by lightning. Then a grim, purposeful voice reassured him.

'Drop that gun. I've got you covered.'

With a snarl of rage, the man with the hidden face swung round. Standing in the doorway, with one hand on the electric light switch, was the stocky figure of Detective Inspector Drizzle — and in the other hand was a large, wicked-looking automatic pistol.

The man with the hidden face cursed. 'You!' he gasped. 'What are you doing here?'

Mr. Drizzle didn't answer, but advanced further into the room. Sergeant Ansell followed him, accompanied by two brawny young constables.

'The game's up,' said Mr. Drizzle. 'Are you coming — '

The man with the hidden face shot a quick glance round the room. The next second he made a dash for the door, sending Sergeant Ansell spinning.

'Stop him!' yelled Mr. Drizzle. 'For Pete's sake, stop him!'

Mr. Drizzle was first out on the darkened landing, and he ducked as a bullet went whizzing past him. He made a frantic dive at the fleeing figure that raced along the landing, and the two of them went down with a crash. The firearms clattered somewhere on the carpet.

Struggling desperately, the figures

scrambled hastily to their feet as someone switched on the landing light. Mr. Drizzle felt two powerful hands encircle his throat, and he gasped. He felt a horrible choking sensation as he tried to wrench them free, but the grip grew tighter and tighter. His head began to swim, and he became vaguely conscious of wild, frantic shouting. Then in a last desperate effort, he swung his fist into that fantastic mask of black silk, and the figure went reeling backwards. There was a sudden awful cry and a series of terrific thuds as the man with the hidden face fell backwards down the stairs. He fell with a crash near the front door, writhed convulsively for a second or two, then lay deadly still.

Mr. Drizzle passed a shaky hand over his tingling throat. 'You all right?' asked Ansell at his elbow, and Mr. Drizzle nodded.

'Yes, I'm all right,' he said. 'But — but I don't think — he — is. I — I believe he's — broken his back.'

Quickly they descended the stairs, and as Mr. Drizzle turned that still body over, his suspicion was confirmed. 'He's not dead,' he sighed. 'But he will be within a few minutes. Spine snapped like a matchstick.'

'Good heavens!' gasped Phillip Manton, who had been released by a constable and was now coming down the stairs. 'But — but who on earth is he?'

'Don't you know?' asked Mr. Drizzle. 'He's a very old friend of ours — or was.'

And as Mr. Drizzle pulled off the black silk face covering, Phillip Manton stared down at the evil, pain-contorted features of — Grasset!

23

The Story

'Newspaper men,' said Mr. Drizzle as he carefully lighted his pipe, 'are a confounded nuisance. How the deuce they got wind of this business I don't know. I've been pestered to death with them all day. If I've told the story once, I've told it a dozen times, and — '

'And now,' remarked Phillip Manton with a grin, 'you're going to tell it again. We're simply dying to hear all about it, and you did promise, you know.'

'Did I?' Mr. Drizzle sighed, and glanced at the cheery little party that was gathered round the cosy drawing-room fire at Friar's Lodge. His eyes rested for a second on Margery, and as he looked at her now he found it incredible to believe that it was only yesterday since the murderer of her uncle had been brought to book; the change that had come over her had been nothing short of miraculous. 'Yes, I suppose I did.' He settled himself snugly in the depths of the massive arm-chair and pulled contentedly at his pipe. 'Where shall I begin? At the beginning? That's the usual place, I believe.'

Margery, curled comfortably on a pouffé, smiled. 'That depends,' she contended, 'on what you call the beginning. If you mean the time when the diamonds were first stolen, yes.'

'All right.' Mr. Drizzle flicked a spent match in the direction of the hearth and drew hard on his pipe till the bowl warmed to a ruddy glow. 'Tell you what; unless you both want boring to tears, you'd better both ask me what you want to know. It'll be quicker that way, and we shan't cover any stale ground.'

Phillip nodded and drew his chair nearer the fire. 'All right. Here you are, then. Ignoring the fact that ladies generally come first, here's one. We know the details of the robbery — you told us that before — but what we don't know is this: What part did Margery's uncle take in it? Was he very important?'

Mr. Drizzle shook his head. 'I don't think so,' he replied. 'In fact, I doubt whether he ever saw the diamonds at all, let alone touched them. But whatever part he took, there seems to be no doubt about him being an unwilling accomplice — the very fact that he came to Enderby for the purpose of recovering the stones to return to their original owner proves that. You see, like most young men of his time, Matthew Trevelyn was inclined to be rather wild, and I'm afraid not at all particular about the company he chose. There's no need to say, however, how much he regretted being mixed up with Fairlie and his brother.'

Phillip nodded. 'And who was actually responsible for hiding the stones?' he asked.

'Lew Fairlie,' replied the Scotland Yard man. 'But that wasn't the original plan, you know. You remember that when the alarm was given at Hereford Hall, the three of them decided to break up and meet again later. Well, Fairlie took charge of the diamonds, and it was while he was hiding in Briar Cottage that he conceived the idea of hiding them. He knew that capture could only be a matter of time — they hadn't bargained on the alarm being given so soon — and he wasn't going to take any chances of the diamonds being found on him.'

'I see,' said Phillip. 'Then I suppose Briar Cottage must have been unoccupied at the time.' He smiled. 'I little knew I was sleeping over twenty thousand pounds' worth of diamonds. I might not have been so considerate towards my public if I had. But what happened then? After he'd hidden the diamonds I mean.'

'They were caught,' replied Mr. Drizzle. 'Trevelyn and Fairlie within an hour of each other. But the diamonds — there was no trace of them, and in the circumstances, it was only natural for the police to assume that they were in possession of the other one. And as Fairlie's brother was never caught . . . '

Margery frowned. 'Do you mean that — that Grasset was *really* Fairlie's brother?' she asked.

Mr. Drizzle nodded. 'He was, and the worse of the two.'

'And what happened to them, then?' asked Phillip. He took out a cigarette and began to tap the end of it on his thumb-nail. 'The two who were caught, I mean. They were sentenced to ten years, weren't they?'

Mr. Drizzle expelled a thick cloud of tobacco smoke into the room and nodded. 'Yes. But they didn't stay there for long. Three years later they made a desperate bid for freedom — and incidentally supplied the papers with another sensation.' He sighed. 'Fairlie was shot while trying to escape. Trevelyn, however, got clear — but not before Fairlie had revealed to him the hiding place of the diamonds.'

Phillip raised his eyebrows. 'You mean that Margery's uncle hadn't known?'

The inspector nodded. 'Fairlie, up to then, had kept his secret entirely to himself.'

Phillip fumbled for his matches and struck a light. He lighted his cigarette, then threw the match into the fire. 'And what happened to Margery's uncle after he'd escaped?'

The Scotland Yard man shrugged.

'That's something I can't really tell you,' he replied. 'You must remember that the war was on then. My opinion is that he enlisted for service in the forces and was sent over to France. Men were being accepted without question, you know, and — well, it's the surest way of evading the police I can think of.'

Margery sighed. 'Poor Uncle. He must have had a dreadful time. I wonder what he felt like when he came back to England.'

'Same as he felt before he left it,' was Mr. Drizzle's convinced reply. 'Determined as ever to return the diamonds to where they belonged. That was why he risked so much in coming back to the district in which he'd been captured — and that was why he lived such a quiet and secluded life.'

Margery nodded and transferred her gaze from the warm depths of the fire to the blue haze of smoke that enveloped Mr. Drizzle's head.

'Then Grasset came and spoiled it all,' she remarked. She frowned. 'I wonder how he knew where Uncle Matthew was living?'

Mr. Drizzle moved his pipe vaguely. 'I can't tell you. And in any case, it doesn't matter much. He did find out, and that's all there is to it.'

'Yes, but — but why on earth did he get himself engaged as butler? Was that necessary?'

Mr. Drizzle nodded. 'It was. He wanted to find out what had become of the diamonds, and the only way he could do that was by getting in close contact with your uncle. You see, Grasset — we'll call him Grasset for the sake of clarity — Grasset knew quite well that the diamonds must have been hidden some-where, but whether they were still hidden he didn't know. And in any case, that didn't matter. Grasset was after some money, and he wasn't particular whether he got his share of the actual stones or his share of the proceeds.'

'I see,' said Margery. She looked at Mr. Drizzle with a frown. 'But — but why didn't Uncle recognize him?'

Mr. Drizzle smiled. 'Twenty-five years is a very long time, my dear, and Grasset had changed quite a lot.' He shook his head. 'No, there seemed little chance of that — at the beginning, anyway.'

'At the beginning? What do you mean? Do you mean that Uncle *did* recognize him?'

'After a time — yes. That's why he left that message.'

'I see. But — but what did Grasset do?'

'Before he was recognized? Discover all he could about the diamonds. In some way he found out that they were still hidden — and that your uncle knew where. Consequently, he indulged in a little blackmail.'

Margery gasped. Her eyes sparkled.

'You mean — ?'

'Exactly.' Mr. Drizzle nodded. 'Those letters you said he used to burn; they were from Grasset — though I'm certain he had no suspicion of that at the time. Grasset threatened to expose your uncle as an escaped convict and as one of the men connected with the Hereford Diamond robbery if he didn't tell him where the diamonds were hidden.'

'And did he?'

'At first, no. But eventually there was

nothing else for it.'

Phillip grunted.

'But that's no reason for him being killed,' he pointed out, and the Scotland Yard man smiled.

'Isn't it?' Mr. Drizzle shook his head. 'There were several reasons for that, you know. One was that Miss Trevelyn's uncle was beginning to get suspicious. Grasset knew this — and he knew also that once he had got the diamonds, Mr. Trevelyn might prove a rather uncomfortable danger to him.'

'But surely Margery's uncle could hardly expose Grasset without incriminating himself,' argued Phillip. 'At least, if that's what you mean.'

Mr. Drizzle shrugged. 'You must remember that Mr. Trevelyn was getting on in life,' he said, 'and though he was by no means an old man, the best part of his life was over.'

'Well?'

'Well, don't you see?' said Mr. Drizzle. 'There was no telling what he might do. At all events, it was too much to risk — and the very fact that he wrote to

Scotland Yard proves that. Besides — ' He pointed the stem of his pipe in Phillip's direction. 'It served quite another purpose.'

'Oh?' The young writer looked up. 'What?'

'It would, in all probability, have been the means of getting you out of the way.'

'Getting me out of the way?' Phillip stared. 'But — but whatever for? I mean — '

Mr. Drizzle stretched his feet before the crackling flames and glanced at Margery over the top of a pair of invisible spectacles.

'Because he was in love with Miss Trevelyn,' he replied.

Margery crimsoned and looked decidedly uncomfortable. 'But that's absurd . . . ' she began.

'Is it?' asked Mr. Drizzle. He drew a long breath. 'Well, you heard for yourself what Grasset had to say about that. It seems impossible in a man like him, I know, but you must remember that he was only human, and — ' His eyes sparkled. ' — you are a bit of a temptation, you know.'

'I mean, why did he want to get rid of Phillip?' she said hastily, and Mr. Drizzle smiled.

'Surely you can see that? Or — ' He glanced suddenly across at the young author. ' — hadn't you ever thought of him that way?'

'Eh?' Phillip eyed him suspiciously. 'What way?'

'As the 'other man',' said Mr. Drizzle. 'Don't you see, Manton? You were in the way. You were in love with Miss Trevelyn, and she was in love with you, and while you continued to exist there seemed little or no chance of Grasset ever making an impression on Miss Trevelyn. So you *had* to be eliminated.'

'Of course.' Phillip gazed intently into the fire. 'Two deaths would have looked a bit suspicious. So he framed the murder on me, eh? Pretty cute, I admit. Sort of killed two birds with one stone. Instead of killing me, he killed Margery's uncle, and let me take the rap for it. But — ' He looked up with a frown. ' — how did he work that? I mean, the scarf — ?'

Mr. Drizzle placed his pipe on the arm

of the chair and leaned slowly forward. 'I know that seems quite a complicated affair,' he remarked, 'but actually it isn't. I work it out something like this: In order to incriminate you as being responsible for the death of Miss Trevelyn's uncle, Grasset had to provide you with some kind of motive. Any motive would do, so long as it was sufficiently feasible. Well, the only thing to do was obviously to promote bad blood between you both, and to do that he engineered the quarrel.'

'Engineered the quarrel?' Phillip stared incredulously. 'But how — '

'By giving Mr. Trevelyn the impression that you were in league with him, that's all.'

'In league with him? But . . . ' Phillip stopped. 'You mean that he thought Grasset and I were . . . were accomplices?'

Mr. Drizzle nodded.

'Well I'm damned!' said Phillip. He glanced across at Margery. 'No wonder he went off the deep end when we said we wanted to be married.'

Mr. Drizzle nodded again. 'That was what Grasset intended. By insinuating that you were party to his blackmail, Grasset was certain that you'd quarrel. And you did — sooner than he expected. And after the words that passed between you both — well, anything that happened to Mr. Trevelyn would be immediately put down to you.'

Phillip nodded. 'Yes, I see that. It was damned clever, and I suppose it was made all the more successful when we announced our engagement. Of course that would be the last straw. A blackmailer in the family . . . But about the scarf. How did he get hold of it? I mean, it was left at Briar Cottage, and — '

'Exactly. That's how. Do you remember what occurred when you came in — before the quarrel, I mean? You met Grasset in the hall, and Miss Trevelyn happened to mention that she had left her scarf at your place and would he ask Ann to get her another — at least, according to one of your servants, anyway.'

'Yes.' Margery nodded. 'We did meet Grasset, and I believe I did ask him. And Ann or someone was in the hall at the time, too.'

'Well,' continued Mr. Drizzle, 'that was just the chance Grasset was waiting for. He knew that you were writing a novel based on a silk scarf crime — he'd often heard you and Miss Trevelyn talking it over in this room, you know — and he saw at once that if Mr. Trevelyn was murdered in exactly the same manner as in your story — a story that had never been published — and with a scarf that had last been in your possession . . . well, you'd obviously have to answer some very nasty questions.'

'Ye-es.' Phillip pursed his lips. 'But how did he get the scarf, I mean?'

'Oh, that was simple,' replied Mr. Drizzle. 'He merely broke into Briar Cottage that night and took it.'

Margery gasped. 'So that was it? And I thought at first — I suppose it was he who told the servants they could have the evening off, wasn't it?'

The Scotland Yard man nodded. 'Yes. Grasset experienced little difficulty in getting the servants out of the way. Of course they thought the order came from Mr. Trevelyn.'

'Yes, but look here. What about Margery?' put in Phillip. 'Wasn't he taking a risk? I mean, what if she'd turned up?'

'That,' said Mr. Drizzle, 'would have been awkward. But Grasset knew quite well that she wouldn't.'

'How could he know that?' asked Margery.

'Well for one thing,' replied Mr. Drizzle, 'you'd been out most of the day, and for another, he knew from what Mrs. Garvice had said when she called that you were likely to be out for most of the evening, too. Mrs. Garvice wanted you to call at Mr. Gregg's shop some time during the evening, didn't she? Well, that was enough for him.'

Phillip nodded and stared hard at the glowing end of his cigarette. 'And how did he commit the murder?' he asked. 'I mean, it looked so much like an outside job — from what I've heard, anyway.'

'Of course it did,' said Mr. Drizzle. 'Grasset meant it to. That was the whole object. With the servants out of the way, he had complete run of the house, and there was no one to dispute that theory.

All that tale about Grasset reading in the kitchen and hearing someone on the stairs was rot. Certainly Mr. Trevelyn did come downstairs, but Grasset didn't go through to him then. He let him get on with the work.'

'What work?'

'The job of preparing the instructions for finding the diamonds,' answered Mr. Drizzle. 'That was why he got up. It had been previously arranged that he should hand them over that night.'

Phillip nodded. 'I see. And then what happened?'

'Grasset waited until he'd written the paper, sealed it in an envelope, and then — then killed him.'

Margery shuddered. 'And I suppose,' said Phillip, 'it was he I ran into on the terrace?'

'Yes,' replied the inspector. 'I imagine you'd give him as big a shock as he gave you. Of course, he must have heard your knocks and rings at the front door, but — well, as he didn't answer them, I suppose he'd conclude that whoever it had been would have gone.'

'Then — what was he doing at Briar Cottage that night?' asked Phillip. He reminiscently fingered his now un-bandaged head. 'Looking for the diamonds?'

'No,' said Mr. Drizzle with a smile. 'He hadn't the least idea where they were then. He was looking for the letter.'

'The letter?'

'Yes. The one Mr. Trevelyn had prepared for him. You see, he dropped it on the terrace when you ran into him, and he was certain afterwards that you must have picked it up.'

'So he recognized me, did he? Well that's more than I did him.' Phillip frowned. 'But how on earth did he get into the cupboard afterwards? And who tied him up?'

Mr. Drizzle smiled. 'That was, I think, the greatest mystery of all. Of course, it suggested an accomplice, but nobody tied him up.'

They both stared. 'Nobody tied him up?' said Phillip. 'Then how — '

'Ever been to a circus?' asked Mr. Drizzle. 'Either of you?'

'A circus?' echoed Phillip.

'Yes. I used to go dotty on 'em when I was a kid, but since then I've risen to a higher standard of intelligence. Anyway, I remember once being awfully thrilled by a chap who trussed himself up with rope in about three minutes, and got free again in about three seconds. Well, that's what Grasset did — only he didn't attempt to get free again.'

Margery gasped. 'You mean . . . actually tied himself up . . . ?'

'That,' said Mr. Drizzle with a smile, 'is exactly what I do mean. It's not very difficult when you know the art. It used to be quite a favourite on the music hall and in circuses, and I really ought to have seen it at first. I suppose it was because it was too obvious that I didn't. Anyone could have got out of those knots in a few seconds if they'd tried.'

'But the cupboard!' said Phillip. 'It was locked.'

'Of course,' said the inspector, nodding. 'It had to be. But that wouldn't be so mysterious if you'd examined the lock. It's one of those slip variety, like the Yale type. All he had to do was to stand up in

274

the cupboard with his back to the door and draw it to him with his fingers. A sudden jerk, the catch slips, and there you are. I tried it this morning, so I know.'

Phillip whistled. 'I suppose we ought to say he was clever,' he remarked, 'but as usual, cleverness in a criminal doesn't pay. What put you on his track?'

'You did,' replied Mr. Drizzle.

'I did?' Phillip stared at him in amazement. 'How do you make that out?'

'Do you remember what you said when Sergeant Ansell and I interviewed you the morning after you'd been attacked? Do you remember what you said you'd seen — about something very white? Well, that gave me my first clue.'

'Did it?' remarked Phillip, not very impressed. 'Well if that's a clue, I'm afraid I don't see it.'

'Don't you? And you a thriller writer, or whatever distinction that profession of yours is called.' The inspector smiled. 'Think. Something very white. *Something very white*. Well, that could only mean a scarf, a handkerchief, or — '

'Or a bandage,' cried Margery. 'Of

course. Grasset was wearing a bandage that night, wasn't he?'

Phillip nodded. 'Of course. I ought to have known. But — but that wasn't evidence — real evidence, you know.'

'It wasn't,' agreed Mr. Drizzle. 'Not on its own. But when I saw a photograph at Scotland Yard and realized later how much it resembled Grasset — well, I began to feel a little more certain. Then there was the accident at the quarry edge. Although I knew later that it couldn't have been Grasset, I was certain that it was his doing. But it wasn't until last night that I was able to get real proof.'

'Oh? What happened then? I mean, now did you find out for certain?'

Mr. Drizzle picked up his pipe and stared at the half-empty bowl intently. 'Quite a few things happened then, but the thing that really put me on Grasset's track was Ansell's phone call — though I admit I didn't think so then. Ansell phoned to tell me that he had discovered the identity of the man on the terrace, and I can tell you that I didn't receive this news with open arms. It seemed to put the tin hat on everything; wrecked my theory completely. How on earth, I asked myself, did Mr. Balmer come to be mixed up with things? If he was the man on the terrace, what about Grasset? Then I saw one thing. The fact that Mr. Balmer was the man on the terrace didn't make him the murderer — not while I'd got such a perfect case against Grasset. So if Grasset was the man behind the scenes, he was still looking for the clue that led to the diamonds. Whatever this clue was, I hadn't the faintest idea, but it struck me that if Mr. Balmer had been at Friar's Lodge that night, it was quite on the cards that he had gained possession of it. Grasset was just coming down the stairs when I finished my telephone conversation with Ansell, and I knew that he must have heard, and in that case — '

'You mean,' said Phillip, 'that you kept an eye on him?'

Mr. Drizzle nodded. 'It wasn't a nice job keeping watch on the fellow's bedroom in a draughty corridor, but I'm thankful to say that I hadn't to wait long. I saw him leave Briar Cottage, I saw him don that horrid black mask of his, and I saw him go down to the Barrel Inn. I was too late, however, to save Mr. Balmer from a very unpleasant accident. When I got inside the pub, he was gone; he'd slipped out the back way, I believe. Anyway, I wasted most of the time looking after old Balmer. If he hadn't been unconscious, he could have saved me quite a lot of trouble. If I'd known what the letter contained, I could have gone straight to Briar Cottage and nabbed him. As it was, as soon as Balmer came to, all I could do was to go back to Friar's Lodge.'

'But — but how did you come to be out in the car with Sergeant Ansell?' asked Margery. 'I mean, what was he doing here when you got back?'

Mr. Drizzle smiled. 'He was looking for you,' he replied. 'One of the servants had discovered that you'd disappeared and phoned for the police. She'd had toothache, I believe, and had gone past your bedroom and found your door open. Anyway, they fetched Ansell on the scene immediately. I think they suspected Grasset and I had something to do with it, as we were not to be found, either.' He shrugged. 'Anyway, when I got back and assured them that I knew nothing about it, the only thing we could do was to put out an all stations call. It seemed pretty evident then that Grasset had taken you. We were dashing down to the police station when we met you. Do you know, if Grasset hadn't told you that he was going back to Briar Cottage, I don't think we should ever have got him. Still, we did, and that's all there is to it.'

'Yes.' Phillip threw the end of his cigarette into the fire and looked at Margery. 'So I was some use after all. I mean, I did come in handy as a bait.' He yawned. 'Well, I think that just about clears it all, doesn't it?'

'No,' said Margery. 'What I want to know is this: What was Mr. Balmer doing on the terrace?'

'Oh yes,' said Phillip, smiling. 'Poor old Balmer. He's all right, isn't he?'

Mr. Drizzle grinned and rose to his feet. 'Right as rain. It was only a scratch he got when Grasset shot at him — though it might have been worse. Do you know, I believe he's enjoyed the experience. I called to see him this morning and I found him as pleased as punch with himself, despite the fact that you can't see him for bandages.'

'Perhaps,' said Margery. 'But that doesn't answer my question. What *was* he doing on the terrace?'

The Scotland Yard man smiled again. 'I think we ought to blame that detective instinct of his for that.'

'Detective instinct?'

'Yes. Or perhaps we'd better call it curiosity. It doesn't matter which; it all amounts to the same thing. Mr. Balmer, with the rest of the inhabitants of Enderby, had heard all about the quarrel up here; and furthermore, he'd seen Mr. Manton come in badly shaken after his visit here, so when I turned up and asked the way to Friar's Lodge — indiscreetly, I admit — well, I think that must have been the last straw. Anyway, Mr. Balmer's somewhat vivid imagination worked overtime, and I believe he thought I was the mysterious stranger out of one of Mr. Manton's novels, or something like that.

In all events, Mr. Balmer came to the conclusion that there was something fishy going on, and our worthy landlord, determined to find out what it was, decided to begin his investigation at Friar's Lodge. Which, for Grasset's sake, was rather unfortunate, for it was he who threw the plant-pot at him, you know, after he had found the envelope.'

'I see,' said Margery. 'Poor Mr. Balmer.' She sighed. 'I shall have to go down to see him.' She frowned. 'I'm glad it's over. It's been . . . horrible.'

'Horrible?' Phillip smiled. 'If it hadn't concerned us, I should have said it was grand. It's the first real adventure I've ever had. Do you know, I believe it'd make a rattling good novel. Better than the original *Silk Scarf Crime*. I've a jolly good mind to write it — it'd be original, anyway.'

Mr. Drizzle nodded and began to walk across the room. 'I think I should,' he said. He stopped with his hand on the door. 'The royalties would come in pretty handy as a wedding present, wouldn't they?' He smiled as Phillip, to hide his

281

obvious discomfort, rose to stir the fire. 'Anyway,' he continued, 'I've got some writing of my own to do, so you'll excuse me, won't you? Reports and all that sort of thing.' And Mr. Drizzle, who had nothing of the sort to do, passed out of the room.

Phillip, prodding aimlessly at the embers, replaced the poker with a clatter. 'Do you know,' he remarked, 'Mr. Drizzle isn't such a fool as he looks. He's right — about the royalties, I mean. Margery — ' He rose to his feet, his face very red. 'I've been thinking. I asked a — a rather important question some time ago. The answer you gave me — it's still . . . still valid, isn't it?'

'Valid?' Margery looked at him in surprise. She gave a little shudder. 'How horribly official.'

'I mean,' he said desperately, 'you will marry me, won't you?'

He hadn't noticed her rise, but the next second he found her in his arms.

'What do you think?' she asked him, and he saw that her eyes were bright and sparkling. 'It would be dreadful to disappoint Mr. Drizzle, wouldn't it?'

And when circumstances permitted, Phillip agreed that it would.

24

Aftermath

It was some months later when Margery Trevelyn received the letter. It ran:

DEAR MISS TREVELYN,

Thank you so much for your kind invitation. I only regret I was unable to be present at the happy event, but of course, as a writer, your husband will realize no doubt just how much of a Scotland Yard official's time is his own. Allow me, however, to send you both congratulations, and to express my sincere wishes for a happy future.

I do hope you received my gift all right. I thought a silver inkstand would be most original — or should it have been a typewriter?

And if that husband of yours is still intent upon writing about our recent adventures, you might tell him that we discovered who was responsible for my little car accident.

Archie Stilman was sentenced to twelve months yesterday.

Yours sincerely,
SEPTIMUS DRIZZLE.

Margery smiled as handed her back the letter. 'And to think,' she said as she slipped it into the envelope, 'that we never knew his name was Septimus till now.'

We do hope that you have enjoyed reading this large print book.

Did you know that all of our titles are available for purchase?

We publish a wide range of high quality large print books including:
Romances, Mysteries, Classics
General Fiction
Non Fiction and Westerns

Special interest titles available in large print are:
The Little Oxford Dictionary
Music Book, Song Book
Hymn Book, Service Book

Also available from us courtesy of Oxford University Press:
Young Readers' Dictionary
(large print edition)
Young Readers' Thesaurus
(large print edition)

For further information or a free brochure, please contact us at:
Ulverscroft Large Print Books Ltd.,
The Green, Bradgate Road, Anstey,
Leicester, LE7 7FU, England.
Tel: (00 44) **0116 236 4325**
Fax: (00 44) **0116 234 0205**

Other titles in the
Linford Mystery Library:

THE SEVENTH VIRGIN

Gerald Verner

When Constable Joe Bentley rescues what he thinks is a nude woman from the freezing waters of the River Thames, his catch turns out to be an exquisitely modelled tailor's dummy stuffed with thousands of pounds' worth of bank notes. Later that same morning, the dead body of a man is found further downriver. Superintendent Budd of Scotland Yard, under pressure to prevent millions of counterfeit notes from entering general circulation, must discover the connection between the incidents, and stop a cold-blooded murderer on a killing spree.

A NICE GIRL LIKE YOU

Richard Wormser

Lt. Andy Bastian is back for his second scintillating case. This time, he heads a gritting and gruesome search for the man who violated a teenage beauty and left her just intact enough to someday tell the tale. But when his best friend becomes the number one suspect in the case, Andy becomes one of the star legal attractions. Without an alibi, things look bad for Andy's friend — but can Andy offer to help him and keep his integrity intact?

THE BALLAD OF THE RUNNING MAN

Shelley Smith

On the Alps, two schoolteachers discover a gruesome sight — the corpse of a murdered man. How the corpse came to be there is the story of Rex Buchanan and his wife Paula. Rex, a pulp fiction author, comes home one day eager to tell Paula about a fantastic plot for his next novel, *The Ballad of the Running Man*. A man insures his life, and with the aid of his wife pretends to fall ill and eventually 'dies' — but Rex wants them to act it out in real life . . .

THE HANGING HEIRESS

Richard Wormser

Marty Cockren, ex-newspaper man and rookie private detective, is offered the chance to earn big money acting as bodyguard to beautiful young widow Eve Chounet, who is due to inherit a huge fortune from her late husband — though as a caveat, only if she remains alive for thirty days, whilst delivering his portrait paintings to each of his companies. But the principals of some of those companies are hell-bent on her murder, and Marty must use all of his cunning to stay ahead of the individuals involved and keep Eve alive . . .